TWELVE
IS TOO OLD

TWELVE
IS TOO OLD

Peggy Mann

DOUBLEDAY & COMPANY, INC.
GARDEN CITY, NEW YORK

For Betsy

ISBN: 0-385-05099-2 Trade
0-385-05110-7 Prebound
Library of Congress Catalog Card Number 78–14705

Copyright © 1980 by Peggy Mann

1

I tore up the birthday card from Aunt Florence and flushed it down the toilet.

Not because of Aunt Florence. I've got nothing against her. In fact, I like her. She sends me a card every birthday with a check in it to match my age. It was the card I wanted to get rid of. A big card filled with gold numbers . . . 12 12 12 12 12 . . . echoing off the page. Inside there was some stupid verse about in-between . . . almost teen. . . . I tore it up so fast I almost ripped the $12.00 check Aunt Florence had clipped to the back.

I didn't want to be in-between . . . almost teen. I didn't want to be twelve. Maybe I'm strange in that way. All the other girls in my class couldn't *wait* to be done with being eleven, which they all regard as a baby age. But I *like* eleven. You know who you are. And you know where you're at. More or less, anyway.

But twelve was like jumping across a big ditch to land in another world. It was a world with these big question-mark posters. Got your period yet? Had your first high? Are you going out with anyone?

I mean, nothing in that other world appealed to me at *all*. I had four more days left in my life to be eleven. And I didn't want any old card from Aunt Florence reminding me that my time was almost up.

Which is why I flushed the card away.

Then I heard the downstairs door slam. And Mom's voice sounded out. "Gurlllls. I'm ho-oooome." She puts on this phony cheerful voice when something's wrong. Otherwise she just calls up a regular-sounding, "Hi."

I knew something was wrong all right. She'd left around four o'clock—all full of hope. She has a real estate business. If you're imagining some big office full of secretaries and salespeople and photographs of Homes, well—it's nothing like that. Her office is in the Sewing Room of our house. But she does have a private telephone—on top of the washing machine. And she has an answering machine that takes messages when she's not home.

She's trained my sister Linda to answer the Office Phone like a secretary. Linda can have this sexy grown-up voice when she wants to. She's sixteen, but she can sound like thirty. And when she answers the phone and says "Fairbanks Real Estate," it *sounds* like Mom must have an official office and secretary. (It was me that suggested the name for Mom's business. I'd seen Douglas Fairbanks on a late-night movie. And the name just sounded like nice old country homes with fireplaces and shutters and stuff.)

Mom chose real estate after the divorce because, first of all, it was something you could get into without going back to college for more education. And, second, she could arrange her hours to be home when Linda and I got out of school. Or, so she thought anyway.

It turned out that most of the people she had to show houses to were men. The wives looked. But the husbands signed the down-payment check. And naturally they wanted to see before they signed. So they either took off from work early—about four o'clock—or they went on weekends. Which meant that instead of being home when we were, Mom was home when we weren't. Except if Linda or I got sick. Then she'd cancel whatever appointments she had. And she'd stay home with us. She's a very good mother in that way.

Linda used to mind along with me that Mom was out when we were in. But when Steve came into the picture, Linda didn't mind about Mom anymore. In fact, she was glad. It made things much more convenient.

Except when Mom came home unexpectedly.

I wondered whether Linda and Steve had heard the cheery call: "Gurlllls, I'm ho-oooome." Maybe they were too—busy. Or too stoned.

I knocked softly on the door of Linda's room.

No answer. Only Sounds. I mean, there must be *some*thing good about it because all those people go in for it so much. But it sure doesn't *sound* so exactly great. All those groans and moans.

I knocked again, a little louder.

And then came Linda's voice, very disagreeable. "What *is* it?"

"Mom's home," I said.

"Oh, GOD!" said Linda, like how could anyone be so inconsiderate as to arrive home without warning and spoil her nice time.

"I'll try to keep her occupied in the kitchen," I said in a loud whisper.

No answer. But there was some shuffling around inside the room. Was he at least getting ready to leave? Our house has no convenient back stairs or tree outside Linda's window. There's only one way out. The front door. But, luckily (for Linda), the kitchen is beyond the Main Room. Someone can sneak down the stairs and out the front door without being seen by a person in the kitchen.

"I'll try to keep her in the kitchen," I said through the door, louder. "But HURRY!"

"Okay, okay," said Linda. No thanks or anything. Well, I'm used to that. (From what I hear she's no worse than other people's older sisters. Which is about the best you can say for her.)

I ran down the stairs and almost crashed into Mom, who was coming up them. "Oh, *hi*, Mom!" I said, sounding squeaky with surprise. "When did you get home?"

"Just now," said Mom. "I got all the way down to the Grange. And there was a message. Mr. George couldn't make it after all."

The Grange is a nice restaurant-inn where she meets her clients, being as she doesn't want them coming to her house and seeing that her office is only a telephone on the washing machine in the sewing room. And Mr. George is a man in whom she has great hopes. Hopes as a client, I mean. He's loaded. Mom only shows him homes that start at $75,000. She has one at $200,000. And that's what she was going to show him this afternoon. I mean—10 per cent of $200,000—(which is what a real estate agent gets) well, as Mom said, "That would keep you girls in jeans for quite a while."

Mom was all sort of singy when she left to meet Mr. George at 3:30. And here the creep didn't even show up. I was mad at him for disappointing my Mom. And because I now had to make the way clear for Steve to sneak out.

"Mom," I said, excited. "I'm so glad you're home. I want to make something special for dinner and I'm kind of mixed up on the recipe. I need your help."

"What are you making?" she said, trying to sound interested. But not bringing it off very well.

"You'll see!" I ran down the stairs ahead of her. She has a lot of these cookbooks on a high shelf in the kitchen—left over from the days before the divorce when she used to be a wife-and-mother and had time for things like cooking. I took down a fat one which happened to be called *Country Cookery* and quickly opened to a page which happened to read "Dumplings"—just as Mom walked in the door.

"This!" I said. "Feathery Light Dumplings. What I don't get is, what does it mean when it says to—'cut in shortening with pastry blender until mixture is crumbly'? First of all, what *is* a pastry blender? Could we use our regular blender?"

As Mom looked at the recipe I got out the blender, which was stashed away behind a lot of pots. All the pots fell out of the cupboard, which made a big clatter. And the blender would make plenty of noise. I could put it on when I heard Steve tipping down the stairs.

"Look," said Mom, "couldn't we have Feathery Light Dumplings some other time? I'm kind of tired."

"I'LL do it all, Mom," I said. "If you just translate the recipe, a little."

"We could buy those frozen dumplings in the supermarket," Mom said. "You just have to warm them in the oven. They taste almost as good as homemade."

"Mom," I said, "PLEASE. I just have this real *yen* for dumplings tonight. Mom, you should encourage me when I want help with the cooking."

She smiled a little, sat down on the high stool by the kitchen counter, and read over the recipe while I took out bowls and spoons and an aluminum muffin tray. Then I heard footsteps on the stairs—or I thought I did anyway—and I started whirring the blender.

"Turn that thing *off*," Mom said loudly.

"What?" I said, though I could hear her perfectly well.

"TURN IT OFF!" Mom shouted.

So I had to.

Then there was the sound of the front door clicking shut.

"Did someone just come in?" Mom asked. "Or go out?"

"I didn't hear anything."

Mom shrugged and went back to reading the recipe. "God," she said then, "flour, baking powder, shortening, milk, eggs! Maybe I was better off when you were a fiend for TV dinners."

At which point Linda wandered in wearing her bathrobe and in bare feet. She gave me a wink, which Mom did not see. That was my sister's way of saying thanks. It made me feel suddenly close to her and in with her. Which is a feeling I don't so often have.

"What happened with Mr. George?" Linda said.

At least the dumplings had gotten Mom's mind off her disappointment. But now when she explained it to Linda, I could see it settling over her. More than disappointment. A kind of misty depression. Nothing you could see. Her voice and her words were the same. Just something you could sense.

But I guess Linda didn't sense it. She just said airily, "Well, better luck next time." And she went out of the kitchen.

"I have a good idea," Mom said. "Since you have this big yen—why don't you transfer it to a cake recipe? You can make yourself a nice homemade birthday cake. At least, it would make all the mess and the trouble and the ingredients a little worthwhile."

I was glad enough to forget about the Feathery Light Dumplings. Frankly, I found it hard to believe that anyone in their right mind would go to all that tremendous trouble to make six dumplings. However, I *didn't* want to get onto the subject of my birthday!

But Mom kept on about it. "Have you invited the kids to your party yet?"

"No," I said.

"Well, for heaven's sakes," Mom said, "what are you waiting for? Your party's in four days." Then she smiled a little sadly. "In four days you'll be twelve years old."

"Listen, Mom," I said quickly, "I don't want to bother about my birthday this year. Let's just forget it."

"Forget it?" said Mom, very surprised. (No wonder. I always made a big thing of my birthdays in the past.)

"We could all go out for dinner at the Grange," I said. "Just the family." (It sounded strange to say "the family." I hadn't said that since Dad left five years ago when he went off with Diane.)

Mom overlooked this idea as though I hadn't even

mentioned it. She was right. Mom and me and Linda at the Grange wouldn't be too great. There was a new kind of stiffness between Mom and Linda, though I didn't know why. When we all ate together at home it got sort of covered up since Mom was in and out of the kitchen and there was conversation to be made about "Please bring in the milk, while you're up." Or sometimes at dinner Linda would ask Mom for home-work help. But she couldn't bring books along if we went out for dinner at the Grange. There would just be this stiffness. And phoniness of everyone trying to have such a good-birthday time.

"You *have* to have a real birthday party, Jody," Mom said. "You always do. It'll be expected. Corinne already phoned me and asked what you wanted for a present."

"What'd you tell her?"

"I said I didn't have the faintest idea. I told her I'd ask you. What *do* you want, Jody?"

It's strange. I'm not a kid that "has everything." On the other hand, there's nothing much that I really *want*. Except a new bicycle. And I had a little hope that my Dad would answer my hints, in that respect.

"I'll think about it," I said.

"Have you thought about what *kind* of a party you want?" Mom asked.

I knew it was no use to say "No kind." She'd insist that I have a party. Mainly because she likes to feel she's doing All the Right Things in bringing us up—without Dad's help. And having a Twelve-Year-Old Birthday Party would sound to Mom like an impor-tant Right Thing. So, I accepted in myself that I'd have to have a party. And I thought of the least birthday-ish kind I could have. "Maybe I'll just invite a few kids and we'll go to the movies and then come back here for pizza and birthday cake."

"That sounds fine," Mom said. "We can decorate the dining room with balloons and things, like we always do." (We never eat in the dining room anymore, like we did before the divorce. It's too much trouble. We eat all our meals in the Breakfast Nook, right off the kitchen. Since Mom's in real estate she calls all our rooms by these fancy titles. Like—it used to be her and Dad's bathroom. Now it's the Master Bath. Even though there's no more Master in it.)

"Look," said Mom, very businesslike, "first things first. Before you make six fluffy dumplings *or* birthday cake, why don't you go upstairs and phone your friends and invite them to your party?"

"Well," I said, "okay." Mainly I said it because I sure didn't want to be bothered with baking anything, just to cover up for my stupid sister. This seemed a good way out.

"And Friday night," Mom said, "you and I will make a beautiful birthday cake together." She slammed *Country Cookery* shut and put it back on the high shelf.

And I started upstairs to phone kids to come to the birthday party which I didn't even want to have.

2

As it turned out I didn't phone up anyone.

I was sitting at the hall table where our home telephone is. And I was just about to call up my best friend, Corinne, when Linda opened her bedroom door and motioned that I should come on in.

She was smiling a little and she said, "I just wanted to tell you—thanks. Thanks from Steve *and* me. You're a good kid."

I can tell when she smiles in that far-off sort of way that she's stoned. And since I hadn't been stoned yet myself, I had no real way of telling whether it was the pot talking, or my sister. I mean, did she really think I was a good kid? Or just some Stupid. Which is the way she often seems to feel I am.

Anyway, I decided to take her at her word, and I said, with a shrug, "Any time."

Then Linda lay back against the pillows on her floor. She once had a nice couch in her room, but she asked Steve and his friend to carry it down to the cellar. She only kept the pillows. She says it makes her room more Basic. And I guess it does. All she has in her room is a mattress on bedsprings. And a wooden bird cage hanging from the ceiling, with a plant inside it. And a lot of other plants at the window. A few posters on the walls. The couch pillows. And the smell of incense. She burns it so much that it's like part of the room. I often wonder if Mom *knows* why Linda's so big on incense. Because it covers the smell of pot.

"I thought of a real nice present to give you for your birthday," Linda said. "Something *special*."

I suddenly wondered whether I'd end up with *two* new bikes (from Dad—if he'd heard all my hints. And another from Linda). Well, I could always sell one.

"How many hamburgers?" Mom called up from the bottom of the stairs.

Linda made a face. (We're both bored with hamburgers. Mom makes them at least three times a week.) Then she held up one finger.

"Two for me," I called to Mom. "And one for Linda."

"Okay," Mom called back. "Dinner will be ready in half an hour. I hope you don't mind eating early. But I've got a lot of paper work to do."

"That's fine, Mom," I said.

Linda motioned me to close the door of her room and to sit with my back against it. We've done that before. It gives her time to light up a joint and then stub it out quick if Mom is at the door. I act as a kind of human lock. *Really* locking the door might make Mom suspicious.

Since I was sitting there and Linda seemed in a friendly mood, I thought I would have a try at telling her what was troubling me. I mean, she might remember what she felt like when *she* was turning twelve. I didn't consider she'd be much good on advice about most things. But maybe on this she could be of some help to me. After all, only four years ago she was like me. Or *was* she? Somehow, I could picture her only like she was now. Except with long straight hair. Now it's short. And with a flat chest. Now it—isn't.

Anyway, since I'd decided to try, I took a deep breath. And I tried.

"Linda," I said, "did you feel kind of—depressed when you were going to be twelve?"

"Depressed?" said Linda, like the word was some new kind of food and she was tasting it carefully to see whether she liked it or not.

"Yeah," I said. "I mean, that's how I kind of feel when I think about it. *Depressed!*" I hit the word harder—maybe to shake her out of her stoned state.

And it worked. She looked at me. Not through me —like she does sometimes when she's high. "Why on earth should you feel depressed?" she said. "I should think you'd be glad to be twelve. People respect you more. You're not just a little kid. You're—beginning."

"I don't want to begin," I said. "I like being little."

Linda shook her head, like she was puzzled. And it was clear that she had never felt the way I was feeling now. I would have left right then, except I had my job to do—leaning back against the door.

"Are you—scared of growing up?" Linda asked.

I shrugged. "It's just, I don't see anything so great about it. I mean, you get your period. And there are all kind of problems with boys. Either they want you. Or they don't want you. Either way it's a problem. And the girls seem to get more cliquey. And all they think about is clothes and their hair and stupid stuff like that. And cigarette smoking and—I mean, I just don't want to get into all that scene!"

Linda took a deep toke on her joint. Then she looked at me for a long moment. And when she spoke, the words came out very thoughtful and slow.

Like she was giving me a great new world philosophy. "Well," she said, "it's going to come anyway. So you might as well face it. There's nothing you can do about it. Except just face it." Then she took another deep toke on her joint.

And that was it. The advice was over. We both watched as she exhaled the pot smoke slowly.

"Well," I said, "thanks." I stood up, but still with my back leaning against the door.

"I'm glad I was able to help," said Linda. "Help for help, huh, Jody?"

"Sure," I said. "Can I go now? I don't think Mom will be coming in."

"Sure," said Linda. She stubbed out her joint carefully and put it in her cough-drop tin. "I should get started on my homework anyway."

"Me too," I said.

I went back to my room feeling even more depressed than before. And I sat at my desk and opened my history book. We were just beginning Ancient Roman Civilization. Music started up from Linda's room. I knew if I went in there, she'd be lying back against her pillows, listening. She seemed to feel if she said she was going to do her homework, that somehow was the same as getting it done. But her messing up in school was none of my business.

I started reading about the economics of the Roman Empire.

That night Mom came in to kiss me good night, like she always does when she's home. It's nice. I call down, "I'm readddddy." And she calls back up, "Have you brushed your teeth?" And I call down,

"Yes." And then I squirrel down under the covers. And Mom comes in. (I don't know why we keep in that part about brushing my teeth. I got into the habit of brushing years ago. I guess it reminds Mom of how I used to *be* years ago. And it reminds me too.)

But this night when she came in, I wasn't thinking about years ago. I was thinking that since I hadn't gotten any help for my problem from Linda, maybe I'd try my Mom. We're sort of close. But I don't ever really *talk* to her, if you know what I mean. And I don't know why I don't. Except maybe I figure she's got enough problems of her own without having to bother about mine.

Still, this wouldn't be any big burdening problem for Mom. So I said, "Mom, the reason I don't want to have a birthday party is—I don't want to have a birthday. I figure if I don't make a big deal about turning twelve, maybe I could just sort of go on being eleven for a while."

Mom laughed. "Well, if you were thirty-nine and said that, it would make some sense. But *twelve*. What's wrong with being twelve?"

"It's too old," I said.

Now she had a soft smile on her face. She looked pretty. The light from the bedlamp was soft too. It made her look more like a photograph than real.

"Too old?" she said. "What I wouldn't give to be twelve again. And start all over." Then she must have realized it was me we were talking about. Not her. And she suddenly looked at me with all her attention. "Too old for what?"

"Just—too *old!*" I said. "You should see the kids in

my class. They're all twelve and thirteen. Except for me. They think they're so grown up. They're too big for themselves."

"They're just—finding themselves," Mom said.

"Well, that's it." I sat straight up. "I don't feel at all lost. At eleven, I don't. I don't want things to change so that I have to begin *looking* for myself!"

"Jody," Mom said, "you're a very together person. Maybe you can weather all the body changes and all that. Without having it throw you."

"It's not just body changes," I said. "In *your* day maybe that's all it was. But now it's—"

"It's what?" said Mom.

I didn't want to tell her "what." Like I said, she's got enough to worry about. If I started telling her about boys thinking you're "ready" at twelve (not ready for all the way—but for some things, which I sure wasn't ready for) . . . and kids selling pot at our school and thinking twelve is old enough to be a good customer. . . . And cigarettes; some kids in our class smoke a pack a day already. . . . I mean, I don't want my Mom worrying that I'm going to get pregnant or lung cancer. So I didn't know how to explain what I was scared of.

"Look," Mom said. She stroked my hair like she used to do when I was little, "I know I'm not home in the evenings as much as I'd like to be. So I don't have as much time with you as I'd like. But tonight—thanks to Mr. George standing me up—I'm here. I'm listening. I'd like to help. But you've got to try to tell me what's wrong."

So I thought of something that wouldn't worry her. And it was something worrying me. Maybe she'd be of some help. "Well," I said, "my friends are all so boring now. Last year, when they were eleven, they used to be really fun. But now, they're so—*narrow.*"

"Can you be more specific?" my Mom said.

"Well, like I went down to Parsons last Saturday with Corinne." (Parsons is the big department store downtown. "The Everything Place" is their motto. And it's true. You can get just about anything you want there. Like they've got this big Sports Shop with neat ten-speed bikes.) "Corinne and I used to have real fun times when we went there. Like we'd move around quickly and look at everything and talk to people. And ride the escalators and the elevators. And sometimes we'd pretend to be other people shopping at the store. Two twin old ladies. Or roommate career girls. I mean, we'd have *fun!*"

"And now?"

"Well," I said, "*last* Saturday all Corinne wanted to do was diddle around looking at the clothes and the cosmetics and stuff. She's getting like the others. All they talk about is boys and their periods and sometimes they get into some bullshit philosophy. But nothing *fun!*"

"Are you still the youngest in your class?" Mom asked.

I nodded.

"That's it then. You have a different set of interests. But as you get older, you'll begin to be like the others. You'll fit in better. It happens slowly. But you'll see. It'll all work out."

"Okay," I said. "Thanks, Mom. I want to go to sleep now. Good night." And I turned over, away from her.

She kissed the back of my head. "Such big problems," she said. I knew she was sort of laughing at me. But in a nice way.

When she went out and shut the door behind her, I felt worse than ever. Maybe my problems weren't so big—compared to paying the electric bill and all. But the problems were big to *me*. And I had nobody to talk them over with at all.

The next morning I got a real shock. Something, I must say, I wasn't prepared for. I share a locker with Corinne—who has been my best friend since the second grade. We were at the locker, getting out our books for the day. And Corinne said, "Jody, I got my period last night."

I said, "oh." It was more like a sound than a word. Like when someone knocks the breath out of you. I didn't know what *else* to say. So I didn't say anything. I just kept on taking my books out of my locker and putting them in my knapsack, which I carry around with me all day.

But I guess Corinne wanted something more than just "oh." Because she told Kim, who has the locker next to ours. And Kim put her arms around her and hugged her and said, "Oh, I'm so *happy* for you!" I mean, that sounded completely stupid to me. But Corinne seemed to like it. And she and Kim went off together.

I felt jealous. I mean, Kim isn't just "some" girl. She is one of "the" girls. She's very pretty. And that makes everyone like her right away. Boys *and* girls. She doesn't make a big deal of her prettiness. Which

is why girls *can* like her. But mostly what they like is
to be liked *by* her. If you're liked by Kim, you're sort
of "in." If that's where you want to be. Me, I was always satisfied having Corinne as my best friend. Sav-
ing seats for each other in class, and going bike riding
Saturdays and all. With Corinne as my best friend, I
felt I belonged enough. And then I could just go on
about my way, as I wanted to.

But now she was going off with Kim! She had
never done that before. When we got our books in
the morning, we always waited around for the other
one. And then we went upstairs together.

Now I had to go upstairs alone.

At least, I *started* up the stairs alone. Francene
came after me.

Now, I don't say Francene is a pain. She isn't exactly. What she is, is a follower. When she chooses
you, she follows you everywhere. Right into the bathroom, even. I know she likes me, because she's told
me that often enough. But she doesn't follow me too
much because I'm usually with Corinne. And Corinne
knows how to get rid of her. She's not very subtle
about it. She'll just turn around and say, "Francene,
stop *following* us!"

I couldn't ever say that in words—because I feel
kind of sorry for Francene.

It's strange that someone's looks—which they really
have nothing to do with—can make such a big
difference in their life. I mean, here is Kim born very
pretty because of the way some genes and chromosomes fitted together, and right away everyone likes
her because they like to look at her.

And here is Francene, born ugly. And with a body

that doesn't fit with her inside personality at all. Her body is "done," if you know what I mean. She wears a 36-B bra. And she has all this pubic hair. More than my sister does even. She has hips and a small waist. Sort of the shape of a big Barbie doll. If her face was pretty and she was eighteen years old, she'd have it made.

But she's twelve. And her face looks like ten. And she's got these braces. I mean, lots of kids in our grade have braces. But somehow Francene always seems to have this mucky spit around her braces. Maybe she didn't get into too good a habit of brushing her teeth. There seems always to be some little bits of food sticking into her braces.

Her hair used to be nice. Long and straight. But—like most of the girls in our class after they get their period—she had it cut short.

And, like most of them, she had it styled the first time. But none of them can ever keep it like that. They wash it all the time. And blow-dry it into a crisp, in all these wrong waves. In my view, it doesn't look much good on any of them. But on Francene it looks even worse. Her hair is dark brown and wavy and knotty and she's always fiddling with it.

Anyway, as I was going up the stairs from the basement, Francene hurried after me, and she said—of all things—"Are you having a birthday party this year?"

I stared at her. How did *she* know about my birthday?

She answered my look. "I always remember your birthday," she said, "because you're the youngest one in the class and I always think how glad you must be to be getting to the same age as the rest of us."

"I don't know if I'm having a party or not," I said.

She nodded. And she smiled. She always smiles in this pursy-mouth way. Maybe to hide her braces, I don't know. But the smile this time seemed so sort of —sad. And I heard myself saying, "But if I do have a party—can you come?"

"OH," said Francene. "I'd *love* to!" She seemed as surprised by the invitation as I was. And she gave me a whole wide bracey-mouth smile.

I felt glad that I had made her happy. But it was one more good reason for me not to have a party. If I did, I'd have to invite Francene.

When I got to history, there was Corinne sitting next to Kim and talking away to her. And Joseph was on the other side of Corinne. She obviously hadn't saved a seat for me. So I sat down—and Francene plunked down beside me.

I began to feel really worried about Corinne. What would my life be like if I didn't have her for my best friend anymore? And it could happen. She might get so in with the "developed" kids, like Kim, that she wouldn't want to bother with me anymore.

When I say "developed," I don't just mean titties. But that can be a part of it. Those whose titties come out nice seem to have more confidence. But some titties are sort of strange-looking at this age. Doris Oberbeck and I have the littlest ones in the class. Ours are just beginning to perk out. The next step is like Corinne's. They're sort of bottle-nosed dolphin-shaped, and they're at the achey stage she says. Then there are some that look like those cardboard containers for eggs. They plump straight out and they're flat at the top. Some, like Francene's, are huge and all finished. But the worst are where one is bigger than the other. Kim is one of the few that has really nice ones, in proportion to her size and age.

Miss Phelps came in then and, like she always does, said, "Good morning, boys and girls." Then she sits on her desk. Not behind it, like other teachers. But she sort of hikes herself up on it. I guess she feels this makes her more "in" with the kids. But, aside from that, she's a real old-fashioned, all-business, no-pleasure teacher. And as soon as the school bell finished ringing for the start of the first class, she pounced right in with the first question, about the social status of Roman women aristocrats.

Since Corinne and I are so close, we sometimes can tell what the other one is thinking. It's weird. But nice. This time I got a whole long thought which might have been going through Corinne's head right then. It sure wasn't going through my head. I mean, it wasn't anything *I* was concerned with.

I thought of how every ancient Roman girl, aristocratic or peasant or whatever, got her period. Every ancient Greek and ancient Hebrew girl, every girl of every stage in history, in every country of the world, got her period. Right up until today. And they all must have had something of the same feelings about it as we have today. Sort of scared and excited at the idea of now being able to have babies. The sign of being grown up. My Mom told me in her day some girls called it the Curse. Maybe that meant in the olden days it wasn't looked forward to so much. And I knew from biology class that in warmer climates girls tend to get it earlier. At nine or ten. But—despite these kinds of differences—on the whole, it's the one thing that ties girls our age together with every other girl in history and every girl now alive in the world.

It seemed to me quite a remarkable thought, and I looked back at Corinne to see if possibly she could be thinking it. But she wasn't. I saw Kim pass her a note. Corinne opened it, read it. Then she and Kim smiled at each other, together.

I wondered if she was whispering to Kim about cramps. I hoped she wouldn't become one of those "I have cramps" types. I mean some of the girls in my class make this whole big deal about their period. They sort of limp around the gym, or they'll walk around kind of stiff-legged. It's always like, "Oh, I can't go bike riding with you today, I have cramps." I sometimes wondered whether these crampy types really do feel so bad, or whether they just take this way of making the announcement that they had their period. Also, I sometimes wondered what cramps felt like. A stomach ache, or what? I mean, I wasn't dying to experience the sensation. But I was kind of curious about how it exactly felt.

Aside from the cramps, two things seem to happen when you get your period. But I'd already made my mind up that they wouldn't happen to me. One I mentioned before. You get your hair cut. And the other, you suddenly get this big interest in how you look, and what you wear. Usually, of course, they're exactly the same clothes as they were before your period. But you make a big production of how you fit into them. You should see some of the girls in my class getting dressed after gym. They put on their jeans and spend minutes taking their ass cheeks and plumping them into the weave of the pants. And if there's a little bagginess around the hips, they pull out the material and straighten out the seams. I mean, it's so phony.

And the ones who wear *bras*—they'll stand around showing them off while they're putting on their jeans. They wouldn't think of putting on their shirt or sweater *first*. That's another thing some girls seem really anxious for—bras. Even Corinne. She doesn't need one. But finally she mustered up the nerve to ask her mother to buy her a bra. And her mother said, "What for?"

Now, with her period, I guess Corinne will get a bra too. A training bra, anyway.

Luckily, Miss Phelps didn't call on me during history because I wasn't paying the least thought to the ancient Romans. Neither were Kim or Corinne.

Watching them whispering together and passing notes, I suddenly decided I'd *better* have my birthday party. It would be one way of getting together with Corinne without Kim around. Because I sure didn't plan to invite *Kim* to my party!

Luckily, when class was over Kim went off to Spanish—which Corinne and I don't have. We take French. So I sort of hurried up the stairs after Corinne and I said, "Hey, my birthday's Saturday. Can you come?"

"Sure," Corinne said. "What kind of party are you having?"

"I don't know," I said. "Why? Does it make a difference? You want to come or not?"

I don't know why I said it like that. Corinne didn't either. "Why are you being so obnoxious about it?" she said.

I didn't say anything. For the reason that I didn't know what to say.

We reached the third floor and Corinne gave me this long look. Then she said, "Jody, I don't understand you right now."

And she walked off down the hall.

I stood there, looking after her, feeling hollow.

Corinne was leaving me. And I hadn't done anything to show that I still want her. She'd been nice to me. I'd been a bitch to her. First about her period. Now about my party.

I had to try to get her back. I ran after her. "Anyway," I said, "can you come to my party, or not?"

"Okay," Corinne said, with a shrug in her voice.

And she walked on into the French class.

Well, if *that* was the enthusiasm my invitation raised with other kids, it would sure be some rotten party.

3

When I got home that afternoon I heard a familiar sound. I let myself in the front door. (I've had my own key since Mom went to work when I was eight.) Usually I'm greeted by this wall-to-wall emptiness when I get in. The house seems to be twice its normal size. And little sounds seem to be twice as loud as they really are. In fact, they're sounds that I don't even hear unless I'm in the house alone.

Well, you'd think that when I heard human voices in the Living Room, I'd have been happy about it. I wouldn't have to be in the house alone till Linda got home at 4:30. (If you want to know, sometimes when she comes home with Steve and they go straight into Linda's room and shut the door, hardly even bothering to say "Hi" to me, it makes me feel even more lonely than if I'm in the house alone.)

Anyway, who I heard was not Linda and Steve. It was Mom and Dad. And they were arguing—which is why I said I heard a familiar sound. Not that Dad coming to see us is such a familiar occurrence. And not that he and Mom argue when he *does* come. She tends to keep out of the way when he has what they call his Visitation Rights.

The familiar part of it took me back to the days before the divorce when I was really little, and when they seemed to be at each other arguing all the time. Now I got the same kind of sick feeling inside me that I used to get then. I'd want to scream out at them to stop it. But I never said anything. I mean there was enough of loud voices in the house without me adding in. Linda used to shout at them sometimes to SHUT UP! And they'd look at her kind of surprised and Dad would speak severely to her for talking so disrespectfully to her parents. And then he and Mom would keep on with whatever argument they were having—but usually in a softer way, for a while.

The arguing stopped when I was seven and Dad fell in love with his bookkeeper named Diane, and divorced Mom, and married Diane. Now they live in a new brick house in Waterford, three towns away.

I hung up my coat and stood in the hall for a minute, not knowing whether to go into the Living Room or not. They were even arguing about one of the same old subjects that I remember. Money. Which Dad never seemed to make enough of.

"Richard," my Mom was saying, "if you don't live up to your agreement, I'm going to have to take legal measures."

And then my Dad said something which made me feel like I'd fallen through the ice into freezing water. "Look, Connie, I've shown you the books. You have the accountant's word for it. The business isn't living up to my expectations. I've got two mortgages to pay off. And now that Diane's pregnant—"

He went on. But I didn't hear any more. All I heard was that word *pregnant*. That's when I froze inside.

My Dad was going to have a baby with Diane. Which meant exactly one thing to me. The little bit of love he had for his "little girl"—as he used to call me—would be turned onto this new kid he was having with that stupe Diane. And the little bit of time he used to manage to scrape up to see *me* would now be spent in something much nicer. Playing with his baby. I used to be special to Dad because I was his littlest. But all that would soon be over with. Linda would still be what she was. His oldest daughter. But me—I was suddenly kicked out of my place by that one word: *pregnant*. Not the youngest. But in-between. In-between age. And in-between in my Dad's view of me—if he even bothered to have a view of me anymore after the baby came.

Well, all in all, it wasn't too happy an overhearing. But, like I had plenty of practice in doing when I was seven and less, I pretended I didn't hear anything. I mean, how long could I stand there in the hall? So I yelled out cheerily, "Hi, Mom," as though I'd just opened the front door.

And my Mom called back, "Hi, dear. How was school?" Then she came into the hallway and she said, "Jody, your father's here. I have to go to the supermarket. Keep him company till I get back." She sounded very angry. And she left, closing the door hard behind her.

I went on into the Living Room as though I hadn't noticed anything wrong with Mom, and I said in a surprised voice, "Hi, Dad, what brings *you* here?"

And then I saw what maybe brought him. There were wrapped-up packages on the coffee table. Three of them.

Dad smiled. "What do you think brings me here! My little girl's birthday. Although you're not such a little girl anymore. Twelve years old. Quite a young lady!"

"Well, I'm not twelve yet, Dad," I said. "I have three more days."

Dad nodded. "I know. But I thought I'd bring your

presents over today because Diane and I are going away over the weekend so I won't be able to come on Saturday."

Since I didn't know what to say to that, I didn't say anything.

"Would you like to open them now?" Dad asked.

"Sure," I said. "If you want me to."

"Go ahead," Dad said.

At least it would give me something to *do*. I often found it hard to think up things to say to my Dad. And he wasn't usually very helpful about thinking up subjects. But opening presents isn't too bad a way to spend your time. I was still angry at my Dad for coming here and upsetting Mom and for displacing me, by having a baby. Even so, I felt kind of excited when I sat on the couch and took the first present on my lap. "It's wrapped up so nice," I said. "It looks too pretty to open."

"Diane wrapped it," Dad said. "She's a good little wrapper."

I tore the paper off.

It was a manicure set. "Oh, that's neat, Dad," I said, trying to sound as though I liked it. I mean, what am I supposed to do with a *manicure* set? Still, to be polite I took out all the little bottles, and read the labels. "Cuticle remover? Aren't you supposed to have cuticles?"

"Search me," Dad said. "I'm no beauty expert." Then he added in a kind of lame way, "I thought you'd like it."

"Oh, I do, Dad," I said quickly. I could always wrap it up again and give it to Linda for Christmas.

At least that would save me some money. I was sorry I'd torn Diane's nice gift paper.

I opened the next present more carefully. It was a blouse. Sort of a smoky blue color. "Oh, this is nice, Dad," I said. It was. Except it had these little seamed places for titties. I always avoid clothes with those seams. What's the point in having these two little sticking-out puffs with just air inside?

"Where'd you get it, Dad?"

"A very posh shop in Waterford," Dad said. "It was hard to know what to get you for presents this year. I didn't know whether to get clothes for you or your Barbie doll. But I figured by now you'd have your Barbie dolls put away. Was I right?"

If he'd been around a little more, he'd have known I never did play with Barbie dolls. I gave him a smile and a nod by way of answering.

"Dad," I said then, "don't tell Linda or Mom you gave me a manicure set."

"Why not?"

"Just don't," I said.

He shrugged. "Well, okay. You girls have secrets we men don't understand."

There was one present left. It was the biggest. And the heaviest. It rattled a little. I couldn't *imagine* what it was. I opened it very carefully, slitting the Scotch tape with my fingernail so I wouldn't hurt the gift-wrap paper. This present would *have* to be something I really wanted, without even knowing I wanted it.

"Is this my main present?"

Dad smiled, and nodded.

Very carefully I took off the paper. A brown wooden box. What on *earth?* I lifted up the lid. A set of oil paints in fat tubes. A wooden palette. Brushes. A bottle of linseed oil. A bottle of turpentine. It was nice. There was only one trouble. I didn't like to paint.

"Do you like it?" Dad said.

"Sure!" I said. "It's neat. It must have been very expensive."

He seemed pleased. "I didn't know what to get you for your main present—until you sent me the Xerox of your report card. You got such a good report in art that—well, I suddenly knew what to get."

"Thanks, Dad," I said. If he only knew—Miss Kennerly, our art teacher, says just about the same thing for everybody. She figures every kid, whether they do good or bad in their regular classes, should have some bright note. Which she can easily supply. So she writes these glowing things about the kid's fine sense of space and how creative they are and the understanding of perspective and the color sense and all that. For the few really good artists in our class Miss Kennerly practically has to turn cartwheels with words, so their reports will sound even better than all the glowy things she writes for the rest of us.

"Of course," Dad said, "it wasn't just the art teacher's report I was proud of. Your whole report card was wonderful, Deedee."

I looked up at him. It was a name he hadn't called me for a long time. It was a name I'd made up for myself when I was a baby and couldn't say Jody. I liked him saying the name better than him giving me the oil-painting set. My little-girl name. Then I remembered that I wasn't going to be his little girl much longer.

"When is the baby coming?" The question was out before I even knew I had thought of asking it.

"Baby?" Dad sounded kind of surprised.

"When I came in I heard you telling Mom that Diane was pregnant."

"Oh, yes," Dad said. "Right. Well—in about four months."

"Oh," I said. "That's great."

"Yes, we think so too," Dad said.

He had been standing up, watching me open my presents. Now he sat down in the armchair. And I stayed sitting on the couch. I hid the manicure set under the pillow so Linda wouldn't see it when she came in. And I noticed that, luckily, the oil-paint set had the name of the Waterford store on a little round label pasted on the box. Maybe I could take the bus over there one day and change in the set for cash. Maybe it would be enough cash for me to buy a ten-speed bike. I hoped that oil paints were very expensive.

"How's school?" Dad asked.

"Fine."

"History still your favorite?"

"I guess."

"What kind of history is it?"

"Right now we're doing Ancient Rome."

We always have these so-called conversations. Like two almost-strangers. Playing Ping-Pong with sentences.

After some more of this I saw him glance at his wristwatch. I said, "You have to go, Dad?"

"No!" he said. "I came all this way to see my girl. I'm certainly not going to go yet."

"Oh, good," I said.

Then Dad thought up another Subject. "What about your friends? Do you still see that Corola, or whatever her name is?"

"Corinne."

"Is she still your best friend?"

"Yeah. I guess. She's coming to my party."

"Oh! You're having a party. Tell me about *that*."

"Well," I said, "it won't be anything much. Probably we'll just go to the movies and for a pizza."

"Well, that sounds good," Dad said. "Are you having boys at your party. Or—just girls."

"Just girls. I'm not that big yet."

"That's good," Dad said. "I think of you as my little girl."

"You *do?*"

"Yes," Dad said.

Suddenly I had this strange wish. I wanted to crawl into his lap and have him hold me. I wanted to *be* a little girl. Deedee. I wanted it to be the way it used to be, long ago. And yet I didn't really want that. Because it didn't used to be too good, as I remember.

The feeling went away very quickly. And we just looked at each other. I thought, *My God, what are we going to talk about now?* I couldn't think of a thing.

Luckily then, there was the sound of a key in the front door. And Linda came in.

"Oh, hi, Linn!" I called.

Then I heard Steve's voice, mumbling something.

Dad called out, "Is that my big girl?"

And Linda came into the room. (If you think my Dad is not too great about making conversation, you should hear Steve. Actually, there's nothing much to hear. He hardly talks. Except with Linda. With other people he likes to stay out of the way. In the next room, if possible. I don't think my Dad even knew he was there in the house.)

"What are you doing here, Dad?" Linda asked. She gave him a sort of kiss on the forehead.

"I came to see my girls. How you been, Linn?"

"Well, listen, Dad," Linda said, "you going to be here for a while?"

"Sure," Dad said.

"Great!" said Linda. "Because Steve stopped over to help me with my algebra. We've got a test tomorrow. So since he has to leave soon, I better go—" She left the sentence hanging.

Dad picked it up. "I'll be here. I'll wait. I don't want to interfere with anything."

I gave a little soft snort under my breath. Interfere! I doubted very much that it was algebra he'd be interfering with. It was the first I ever heard that Steve knew one thing about math.

"Great!" Linda said again. "I'll be down soon."

And before I knew it she was gone—up the stairs with Steve. And I was still sitting there stuck with him and not knowing what to say.

Suddenly I *saw* him. It was as though a see-through plastic shade had been hanging in front of him. And it was snapped up. And there he was. Clear. Kind of stringy hair. Blue blazer, with the brass buttons. No tie. Collar open. A gold chain around his neck. Dark chest hair showing through. His looks had changed since he'd married that stupid Diane. He was trying to be so cool.

It was so weird. He was like a complete stranger,

sitting there. And yet he was my Dad. My flesh and
blood. I'm made out of half of him. Without him I
wouldn't be sitting here. Without him, I wouldn't *be.*
And yet, who was he? I didn't know him. And he
surely didn't know me. We just didn't have a thing to
say to each other.

Then, suddenly, I thought of a Subject. "How's
your business, Dad?"

He had been in Men's Wear, Retail. But when he
and Diane moved to Waterford he sold the shop and
he and Diane went into a new business. Cheese. I
know it sounds funny. Some words just sound funny,
all by themselves. Cheese is one of them. But the
shop is nice, actually. It has this fancy sign out front:
Cheeses of the World. It was Diane's idea. She
wanted something that she could be in with him, as
equal partners. And Men's Wear, Retail didn't fit that
requirement so well. Diane's a real cheese freak. And
she figured imported cheeses are one thing you can
never get in the local supermarket. So she and Dad
opened this sort of gourmet shop in Waterford. The
only trouble is, there don't seem to be too many other
cheese freaks in Waterford. At least, not freaky
enough to spend all the extra money that imported
cheese costs.

The last time Dad talked about his store, he
seemed kind of up about it. He told us how it was
drawing in a better class of customer from other
towns in the county. Like a better mousetrap, he said.
(At that point I'd wanted to make some joke about
cheese and mousetraps. But I couldn't think how to
put it together, so I hadn't said anything. Which was
probably just as well.)

Now when I asked about his business, Dad only

shrugged. "Well," he said, "it's chugging along. It could be doing better."

"I'm sure it'll *get* better, Dad," I said politely.

"Well, I certainly hope so," he said. "Because your mother seems to—"

There was this silence.

"Seems to what?" I asked.

"Nothing," he said. "Nothing."

Well, there went another Subject.

"Would you like something to eat, Dad?"

"No, thanks." He looked at his watch again.

And I looked at my presents. Suddenly I had this vision. Diane was cooking at the stove in their nice new kitchen. And Dad walked in and said to her, "Oh, gosh, Jody's birthday's coming up. Diane, would you pick up a few things for her on your way home?"

I stood up. "Dad, I'm really, really sorry but I have a really, really lot of homework to do. So I really should go up and do it now. I'll send Linda down to talk to you."

Dad looked at me. I couldn't tell if he felt insulted, or relieved. "Okay, Deedee," he said. Then he stood up. "I know that you're a hard little worker. And I want you to know I'm very very proud of your report card." He put his arms around me and kissed the top of my hair. When I suddenly lifted my head to kiss him, his jaws sort of clanked together.

"I'm sorry, Dad," I said.

"For what?"

"I thought I might have hurt you with my head."

"You didn't hurt me," he said.

I kissed his cheek. Then I picked up my presents. "I really, really love what you got me," I said.

"I wish you a very happy birthday," he said in a

formal way, as though he was reading the print on a birthday card.

"Thanks, Dad," I said. "For everything."

He nodded. "That's okay," he said. " 'Bye 'bye, Deedee."

As I walked up the stairs carrying my three presents, I felt sadness coming from some deep place inside me. But I didn't really know what I was so sad about. Or why I was starting to cry.

4

I put my presents in my room and hid the manicure set under my pile of underpants. That's the one drawer Linda never looks in to borrow something. She doesn't like the square-looking white cotton underpants that I wear.

Then I knocked on Linda's door.

No answer. Naturally.

I knocked again.

"What?" Very snappy and disagreeable.

"Dad's waiting for you downstairs," I said.

"Can't you see I'm busy?"

"Sure," I said through the closed door. "I know that. But I've been sitting down there for fifteen minutes and I'm out of subjects."

"Fuck," Linda said.

"Linda, please. He's your father too."

"All right. All right," Linda said.

She opened the door and came out. Steve was sitting on her bed, rolling a joint. He looked at me without even seeming to see me.

Linda closed her bedroom door, gave me a look for interrupting the proceedings, and started down the stairs. She was wearing shorts and in her bare feet, which I didn't think was too smart being as she had told Dad she was so busy studying algebra. But what she wears is *her* problem.

I went into my room and shut my door. And I tried on the blouse. Hopefully, the seams wouldn't show. But they did, even more on than off. They pucked out like a big announcement that I was still flat. Otherwise the shirt was really nice. It matched my eyes. I wondered whether this was an accident, or whether Dad had chosen the color on purpose. If he *had* picked out the shirt at all. Another little vision came into my head. Diane was saying, "What color are Jody's eyes, darling?" And Dad was saying, "Her *eye* color? I have no idea." And Diane said, "Well, have a look in at them the next time you see her. It would be nice to get her a birthday blouse that matches her eyes."

I took off the shirt and hung it in my closet. It would have to wait there till I could fill it up a little. Hopefully I wouldn't have grown out of it by then, arm-length-wise. I put my T-shirt back on and settled down to do some homework.

About ten minutes later I heard Dad call out, "'Bye, Deedee."

I ran to the top of the stairs. He was just at the front door. I wondered whether I should run down the stairs and kiss him good-bye, or what. But while I was wondering, he waved up at me and said, "Have a wonderful birthday, hon." Then he opened the door and went out.

"'Bye, Dad," I called after him. But I don't know if he heard me.

I went back to my homework, and when Linda came upstairs she ambled into my room. She doesn't come into my room very much—except if she wants me to do something for her.

"Can I see your presents?" she said.

"Did Dad tell you what he got me?"

"I didn't ask him," Linda said.

I showed her the oil-painting set which she thought was neat. "Can I use it sometime?" she asked. "I've thought about going in for art."

"Well," I said, "as a matter of fact I'm planning to return it and use the money toward a ten-speed bike."

"Oh," Linda said. "What else did you get?"

I showed her the shirt.

"It's great," she said, holding it up against her and looking in the mirror on my closet door. "It just matches my eyes. Can I try it on?" She threw the shirt on the bed, and pulled off her sweater.

"Sure," I said.

It just fit her, being as she is small-boned, and slim. Except for her chest. I mean, she has a really nice figure. The blouse with those tittie seams was obviously made for her kind of shape, not mine.

"I have the greatest present in mind for your birthday," she said. She was looking at herself in the mirror again, and I could see that she was smiling a little. But whether the smile was about my great present or about how she looked in the shirt, I couldn't really tell.

"Well," I said, "that's good." I didn't want to get too excited about the present because Linda never has any money. I mean, she *has* money. She gets it from dealing. Except, what she gets, she spends buying more pot. But maybe she'd been able to make a really good buy and she'd sold enough so that she had a good hunk of money left over. Enough for a ten-speed bike. I mean, I hadn't made it any secret how much I wanted a bike.

"It's something I think you'll really like," Linda said.

"Well, *that's* good!" I could hear the hope in my voice.

She turned away from the mirror and she smiled at me again. "You think I could borrow this blouse for Friday night," she said. "Steve and I are going to the disco that just opened and I'd like to wear something nice and new."

I hesitated. "You'll get it all sweated up in the underarms." She'd borrowed a red shirt of mine once, and now it had two pale-red oval patches in the underarms. I felt embarrassed wearing it. My own underarms don't sweat yet. Maybe that's another of the pleasures that comes with Growing Up.

"I promise I won't," Linda said. "And if I do sweat it up, I promise I'll buy you a new blouse just like it."

I didn't count much on that promise. But anyway I shrugged and said, "Well, okay"—partly because if Linda really wants something she always keeps on till she gets it, and partly because I didn't want her to decide not to get me the great present she was planning for my birthday.

"Thanks, Jody," Linda said. "Well, I better start my homework now." And she walked off into her room wearing my shirt. Then she put a record on her stereo, real loud. She always plays it at the top of its voice when Mom's not in the house. I usually don't mind the loudness. But Mom hates it. Linda waits till Mom shouts, "Turn that thing DOWN," and then she softens the volume.

Because of the loud music, I didn't hear the front door open and close when Mom came back. But when there was a pause of quietness while Linda changed records, I heard a very unusual sound. Someone was downstairs—*singing*.

I can't ever remember anyone singing in our house. At least, not for years. In the old days before the divorce Mom used to sing sometimes when she was making dinner or washing the dishes. She used to sing along with the radio, especially if they were playing those old-fashioned Swinging Sixties or Fabulous Fifties songs.

I went downstairs to see who was singing now. And what do you know. It was Mom!

She'd left the house sad and stormy, closing the door hard behind her like a parting insult. And here she was in the kitchen, making dinner—and singing. I wondered what on earth could have happened to change her around. Maybe she'd bumped into Dad and he'd told her he promised to be good about the child-support payments and that he was going to start off his new intentions by buying me a ten-speed birthday bike.

"Well!" I said. "You sound happy."

"Do I?" Mom laughed a little. "How many hamburgers do you want for your dinner?"

I started to say we'd had hamburgers last night, but I decided not to mention it. I didn't want to put her off the track of telling me why she was happy. "So," I said, and I perched myself up on the kitchen stool. "Why?"

"Why what?" said Mom and she started patting the hamburger into patties. "How many? How hungry are you?"

"One," I said. "A cheeseburger—if we have cheese. So what happened when you went out?"

"Nothing happened," Mom said. "I went shopping at the supermarket. That's what happened."

"That's why you suddenly burst out singing?"

Mom looked at me. Then she hugged me. That really surprised me. Something great must have happened. Mom hardly ever just comes up and *hugs* me like that.

"Since you're almost twelve," Mom said, "I guess you're old enough to discuss certain things with."

"Sure," I said, but not sounding too certain about it.

"Remember Mr. Anderson?"

I didn't.

"Clive Anderson," Mom said. "He was a client of mine two years ago. He and his wife. I sold them a house in Clintonville."

"Oh," I said. "Clive Anderson. Yeah." I still didn't remember. But I wanted to encourage her to keep talking.

"Well, I happened to bump into him in the supermarket. Literally. At least, our carts bumped. We were coming in opposite directions and we were each busy looking at the shelf for—" She broke off.

"Yeah?" I said, prompting. "So your carts bumped?"

She laughed a little. "I guess it's not the most romantic way to meet someone. But—" She shrugged, and she kept on patting the hamburgers.

"Is he still married?" I asked.

Mom looked at me. "You *are* growing up, aren't you!"

It turned out I'd said the right thing, because Mom sat down on the other kitchen stool and she opened up like I was a regular friend of hers, instead of her kid. "Not only is he not married anymore, but he's moved back here. He lives in the Shelton Arms. He works for a law firm downtown. Dudley, Finletter, and Anderson. He's one of the partners."

"Great," I said.

"Ah he uh—we uh—"

"Yes?" I said, very interestedly.

"Well, I put our groceries in our car and he put his in his car and then we went into Sloane's for coffee."

"That was nice," I said. I wasn't too sure of myself when it came to carrying out conversation on this Upper Level.

"We got on very well," Mom said. "I mean, I'd always found him an attractive person. Not in *that* way. I mean, I only knew him as someone else's husband. But I always found him very pleasant and interesting. Very intelligent."

I nodded. And waited.

"Well," Mom blurted, "he asked me out tomorrow night."

"Oh," I said.

"We're going dancing."

"Oh," I said again.

"So I thought I'd make your birthday cake tonight. Since I'll be out tomorrow night. Luckily I bought all the ingredients for it while I was shopping."

"Yeah, luckily," I said.

I felt happy for my Mom. Because she was happy. But at the same time I felt kind of surprised and uneasy. You see my Mom hasn't really gone out too much since the divorce. Not that she has anything against it. But, as she's often mentioned, in a town the size of ours there just aren't too many unattached males floating around. Well, there are some; like one of the math teachers in our school. But he's gay. In fact, as far as I know the only time Mom's had a date was when someone's bachelor brother or something like that came to town for a short visit. But I must say, none of these few dates ever made Mom *sing*.

That's why I felt uneasy. What was going to happen now with this Mr. Anderson? Would he step in and take up the closeness that there was between my Mom and me? When I say closeness I don't mean that we tell each other many "inside" sort of things. This conversation we were having on the kitchen stools was the nearest Mom had ever come to that, with me. And last night, when I tried to tell her why I didn't want to be twelve—maybe that was the nearest I ever got about inside things, with her. Still, we are close in that we hardly ever fight. We're very —friendly. I mean, Mom and Linda always seem to be "at" each other. About little things. (The big things that Mom should be "at" Linda about, she doesn't even know about. Pot and what goes on with Steve, and all that.)

Anyway, I suddenly didn't want to hear any more about Mr. Anderson. So I slid off the stool.

But Mom still stayed, sitting. "Jody," she said.

I looked at her.

"In a way I'm sad that you're growing up. I loved having a little girl. But in another way, I'm glad. We'll be able to communicate in—a different way. Do you know what I mean?"

"I guess so," I said. I tried to sound just regular. But it made me feel very down. I was her kid and she was my Mom and I wanted things to stay just that way. I sure didn't want to be turned into any gossip pal for my Mom.

45

"Do you want to help me make your birthday cake after dinner?" Mom asked.

"Well, I'd like to," I said. "But I've got a lot of homework tonight. We have a history test tomorrow and I have to study for it." Actually, I didn't have a history test at all. I don't tell too many lies and I don't know why I told this one—except I felt this big need to be alone now and the history test would give me an excuse to shut the door of my room and not come out again until the morning.

5

By the next morning, thank goodness, Mom seemed to have decided that, after all, I was her kid, not her girl friend. And she didn't say another word about this Clive Anderson.

I'd thought a lot about him during the night. I had him pictured in my mind as clear as a snapshot. Since I'd completely forgotten what the real Clive Anderson looked like I was fresh to do my own imagining. Being as his name sounded like a big game hunter, and being as Mom had sounded so hyped up about him, I imagined him as really tall and broad and handsome; one of these hunters that you see on TV who take people on safaris. I mean, that's basically what he *looked* like. But, being a lawyer, I visioned him dressed in a business suit with a shirt and tie.

I guess Mom had been thinking about him too, because—although she didn't once mention him—she seemed more up than is usual for her in the morning. (She's one of these I-can't-function-until-I've-had-my-two-cups-of-morning-coffee types.)

She began asking me about my party and who I had invited.

"Well," I said, "so far only Corinne. And I guess I invited Francene. Sort of."

"Only *two*?" Mom said. "Jody it's Thursday morning! Your party is Saturday! Don't you realize that?"

"Yeah," I said. "Well, I was thinking I might not even *have* a party. Maybe just I'll go to the movies with Corinne."

"Why on earth would you want *that*?" Mom said.

I shrugged.

"On account of the money? Jody, we may be broke. And it's true that your father hasn't come across with what he owes me. Which is why I can't buy you the bicycle you want. But we certainly have money enough for you to have a party. The movies and pizza and ice cream and cake don't cost *that* much."

"It's not the money, Mom," I said. "It's just—"

"Just what?" Mom reached across the table, knocking over the box of bran flakes. And she put her hand on top of mine. This meant a lot to me being as she just doesn't *do* that kind of thing. It meant she was trying to—reach me. The inside goings-on of me.

I tried to explain. "It's just—like I said, if I don't have a twelve-year-old birthday party to celebrate the great event, maybe I could go on sort of being eleven."

Mom frowned a little. She took her hand away and sat back in her chair. "Jody," she said, "I don't understand. What are you so scared about? Being twelve will be fun. I remember when Linda was eleven. She just couldn't *wait* till her twelfth birthday. She *wanted* to be grown up. Do *you* want to keep on being a baby?"

I shook my head, no.

"Well, then," Mom said, "a nice party will help you get over this foolish feeling. You always enjoy your birthday parties. Now by the time you come home from school today, I want you to have everyone invited. Okay?"

"Okay."

"You don't need to invite the whole *class*," Mom said. "Like you did in the third grade. It took me a week to get the house in shape again after *that* invasion. But invite about six or eight people at least. Otherwise, it won't seem like a real party."

At that point Linda wandered into the kitchen, wearing her bathrobe. Just as if it was a weekend morning. Mom looked at her. "Do you realize what time it is, missy?" she said.

Linda sat down and poured herself a cup of coffee.

"I'm speaking to you!" Mom said sharply.

"I'm aware of that," said Linda.

"Look at you! Still in your robe!"

"Look at you—still in *your* robe!" Linda said.

"I do not have to be in school in thirty minutes," Mom said. "My day doesn't start until eleven o'clock."

"Mom," said Linda, sticking a piece of bread in the toaster, "my first class is English literature. The teacher is a really nice guy and he allows us to be late. Just don't worry about it."

"The report card you just got—and you tell me not to *worry!*" Mom said.

"Stop *hassling* me!" Linda said in a quiet kind of shout.

"It seems to me I don't hassle you *enough!*" Mom said. "Every one of your teachers wrote that you weren't doing as well as you could. Weren't living up to your potential. You're a bright girl, Linda. You used to get A's and B's. Now you come home with C's and D's. And eighteen latenesses last semester. I should think you'd be ashamed enough by that to at least *try* to do better."

I sat there praying hard that she wouldn't say *Look at Jody.* That's all I needed, to have Linda turn on

me. I wanted my sister to like me. I needed my sister
to like me. And the best way to get Linda down on
me would be for Mom to say—

"Look at Jody," Mom said.

Oh, lord!

"—she's dressed and washed, finished her breakfast.
Ready to go."

Linda shot back, "Okay, Mom, you want me to be
like *Jody!* That's the real problem. Never mind my
own personality. Oh, she's all washed and dressed and
ready to pop out the door to school. And I'm not. So
that's my personality, Mom. And if you don't like it,
so just don't accept me. But that's the way I am. I'm
not going to change, I'm not like Jody and I never
will be. So just STOP!" With that she shoved back
her chair, got up from the table, and went upstairs.

Mom and I looked at each other in silence. The
toast that Linda had made popped up in the toaster,
making a sad little sound in the quietness.

Then Mom sighed. A sound much sadder than the
toast had made. "I don't know what's the matter with
her," Mom said. "She used to be such a—a nice girl.
Filled with the joys of spring. Even in the wintertime.
Now she's so—changed. I feel as though there's a wall
of glass between us."

"Maybe it's just—a stage," I said.

"That's what I keep telling myself. But if it is, let's
pray she'll soon grow out of it. I don't know how to
cope with her anymore."

"Listen, Mom," I said, "I better go. Otherwise I
may miss the bus." Actually, I had plenty of time because the bus wasn't due for another ten minutes. But
I felt I'd rather stand by the bus stop than stay here

and maybe get into trouble about Linda. I had my own private ideas on why she'd changed. But I sure didn't want to discuss them with my mother!

Just as the bus came along, so did Linda—running down the sidewalk, waving at the driver to wait for her. He did. And we climbed on together. I hoped that there wouldn't be two empty seats together. But just my luck, there were.

I sat down and Linda sat next to me. Her hair looked the way it had when she got up out of bed. And although she had her various pieces of clothing on, she didn't look very put together. But, on the other hand, that's how she seems to like to look. Which is another big change. Last year she was so *into* clothes. The way most of the girls in my class are now.

Linda opened the conversation. "Mom sure was a bitch this morning."

I didn't want to get caught sticking up for Mom and making Linda even more against me than she already was. So I decided to say straight out what was worrying me. "You made me feel pretty stupid saying all that about me."

Linda looked at me. "I'm not *criticizing* you, Jody. But there you are all ready with your books and washed and all. I think it's very good, but—I'm just very different from you. And Mom compares us. I'm sorry if I made you feel stupid. But it's the only thing I can say to set Mom straight."

"Yeah," I said. "I know." It seemed the best way

to end the conversation. And that is what I wanted to do. "I have this history test—" I said. I opened my book. And we didn't talk any more.

It's not that I didn't want to talk. I felt I had so much to say inside myself. But I had no one to say it *to*. I wished I had just one person in the world that I could talk to about my problems. Corinne used to be the person I could talk to. About just about anything. But now Corinne was one of my problems. And I wasn't close enough to her now to tell her about my other problems. I even had the feeling that if I did tell her some of the things, she might use them against me. Like sort of laughing about me with Kim. She could get more in with Kim by saying how stupid I was about wanting to stay eleven. I mean, I could just *hear* both of them giggling and laughing. Naturally, that made me feel just great—even though I was only "hearing" them inside my own head.

When we got off the bus, Steve was waiting there for Linda. They went off together. I watched them as they walked up the steps to the school. They were holding hands.

I don't like Steve too much, so I never felt jealous of Linda before. But now I did feel jealous. Not because Linda had Steve. But because Linda had her one person. One person she could tell anything to. One person who cared about her—the most. I wondered if I would ever have anyone who loved me like that. Probably I wouldn't.

Maybe I should try to be more *like* Linda. But I didn't know how. It was hard to know where Linda was coming from. Or even where she came from. She wasn't like Mom. She wasn't like Dad. And, as Mom had pointed out, she wasn't even like herself—the way she used to be.

I walked on up the steps, and into school. Some tenth-grader in the hallway asked me if I'd like to buy a "j." But I told him I didn't have a dollar.

"Okay," he said, "so I'll give it to you for whatever you've got. But remember me next time."

"Okay," I said. "I'll remember. But I don't have any money right now. Sorry."

"See you around," he said and he walked off.

Actually, I did have a dollar. My lunch money. Maybe I should have bought a joint. Maybe it would make me feel better. I'd seen plenty of kids get all giggly when they first started smoking pot. If you were giggly you must be happy. And if you were feeling as low as I was, and could buy some happiness for one dollar that wasn't too bad a bargain.

Maybe tomorrow I'd buy a "j." Give myself a birthday present. After all, half my class were already pot smokers. So why not me?

On the other hand, my sister is the biggest pot smoker I know, and in thinking about it, I can't remember her laughing recently. What she seems to be most is disagreeable and kind of down. Maybe it's just when you start that you get giggly.

"HI!" said Francene.

"Oh," I said. "Hi."

"Did you—decide?" she asked.

"Decide?" I knew what she meant, but I pretended I didn't.

"Oh!" I said. "Yeah. Well, I'm not absolutely *certain* yet." A quick look of hurt showed in her face. I knew just what she was thinking: *Jody is having the party. But she doesn't want to invite me.*

"But it's pretty certain," I said. "So why don't you plan on coming—if you're still free. I'll know definitely by tonight. So if I don't call you, that'll mean I'm expecting you."

"Okay," said Francene. I could see she was holding herself back, not wanting to get too worked up about it until she saw whether or not she got the phone call. "If you *do* have the party," she said then, "what would you like for a present?"

"Well—" I said, thinking about it. That was one good thing about birthday parties. The more kids you invited, the more presents you got. At that third-grade party when I'd invited the whole class, I had a whole mountain of presents to open.

"You mentioned you might get a new bike," said Francene. "So maybe I could get you an accessory for it. A night light. Or a bell. Or both."

"Well," I said, "that mightn't be too good. My Mom and Dad seem to be kind of broke this year. So it would be kind of embarrassing for them if I ended up with bike accessories and no bike."

Francene nodded. "My Mom and Dad are kind of broke this year too," she said.

Maybe she was a really nice kid, behind the spitty braces and all. Maybe it was just sort of the *fashion* not to like Francene. On the other hand, if I got too chummy with her, it might also become the fashion not to like *me*.

"Who else might be at your party?" Francene asked. "If you have one."

"Well," I said, "so far I've just asked Corinne and you."

"Really?" She seemed pleased. And proud. Maybe this was the first time she'd been the second person invited to anything.

I saw Andrea down the hall, and I had an idea. "So long," I said to Francene, "See you." And I hurried away.

Andrea Cohen is the most popular girl in our class. She's not the prettiest. She's not the smartest. I don't even know why she's the most popular. But one thing is sure. She is. If Andrea came to my party, she would sort of balance out Francene.

The only trouble is, I don't know her very well. She's got her own group of friends—even though everyone who isn't in her group also likes her. I'm one of those.

Can you just march up to someone who's never set foot inside your house and invite them to something as special as a birthday party? Sure, if you're inviting the whole class—like I did in the third grade (when Andrea was not included, being as she didn't come to our school till last year). But Mom had said invite six or eight kids. And I didn't want any more than that because, at this age, more can suddenly get to be too many.

I decided to settle the question by not thinking about it. I walked up to Andrea, who luckily happened to be alone in the hall for a change, and I said, all in one breath, "I'm having a birthday party Saturday and I really like you even though we haven't gotten to know each other too well and what I wonder is —could you come to my party?"

She looked a little surprised. Then she said, "I really like you too, Jody. And I *would* like to get to know you better. I'd love to come to your party. The only trouble is, I have a date with Roger on Saturday."

"Well—you're welcome to bring him, if he'd like to come." What she'd said had made me feel really happy. *I really like you too, Jody.* "We're going to a movie and then the pizza parlor and then home for ice cream and cake. No big deal, but—" I shrugged.

"That's probably all we'd do on our date anyway," Andrea said. "Movies and pizza. I'll ask Roger. If you're sure you want him."

"Sure I'm sure," I said. "But—I'm only having six or eight people. So keep it private when you ask him."

"I know," Andrea said. "I always try that too when I'm having parties. No need to make a public announcement—so all the people who aren't invited feel bad."

Then a couple of her real friends came up to her. She gave me a kind of nod. A private way of saying "I'll let you know." And she went off with them down the hallway.

I went on into biology class feeling kind of hopeful. Maybe this would be the start, and things would suddenly begin to get a lot better.

Little did I know as I sat in the fourth row and opened my notebook that in the next hour a big *new* problem would fall onto my head!

6

Ms. Cramm is our biology teacher. She's new in the school this year. And, naturally, before we had her we were making up these not-too-great jokes about her name. Ms. Susan Cramm. She's the only teacher who asks her students to call her Ms. Not that she comes on strong as Ms. Women's Lib. But she is kind of with it. In a lot of ways. Sometimes she even wears jeans to class. And when *she* sits on the desk to talk to us it's natural. Not like Miss Phony Phelps.

Ms. Cramm sounds like a fitting name for a teacher. But actually you don't have to cram too much for her tests, because she makes things interesting along the way. So the facts stick in your head very conveniently. She likes to bring in "exhibits" whenever she can. And slides and stuff.

We were studying pollution. We did air pollution. And water pollution. And on this day that I'm referring to we started in on body pollution.

First Miss Cramm held up a big fat book. Exhibit A, she called it. It must have been an inch thick. "This," she told us, "is the Surgeon General's latest report on the health hazards of cigarette smoking. It has summaries of thirty thousand research papers."

Sandy Weatherall, sitting next to me, gave a little sigh. I could hear what he was thinking. He'd just taken up cigarette smoking and he felt real cool about it. He sure didn't want to hear any thirty thousand research papers' worth of what was wrong with cigarettes.

I didn't either, if you want to know.

Not because of my own smoking habits. I tried a few times, but I couldn't seem to get the hang of inhaling. One time I coughed a lot. The other time I got kind of dizzy. So I decided to give it up for a while.

And Linda doesn't smoke too much. I mean regular cigarettes. She more or less gave them up when she started smoking pot. Since pot is harmless, she said, and tobacco isn't—why bother with regular cigarettes?

It's my Mom that I'm worried about in the cigarette connection. After the divorce she took up smoking in a big way. She says it relaxes her. And also it keeps her weight down. One time last year I saw a lot of those TV cancer-cigarette commercials which kept popping up on a series I liked watching. I really kept after Mom at that time, and she did cut down. But she got very cranky. And Linda told me for God's sake to let Mom have her cigarettes so she would stop hassling everyone about every little thing.

Well, now Mama smokes as much as she used to. And if Ms. Cramm kept on about the thirty thousand research reports I'd have something else to worry about Mom-wise. In addition to this Clive Anderson, I mean.

I wanted to tune out on the subject. What you don't know doesn't hurt you. Somebody said that. It may not be very true. But it can be convenient. It's hard, however, to tune out in Ms. Cramm's class because she's one of these teachers who keeps things hopping by springing questions all the time. Sometimes she calls on whoever raises their hand. But sometimes she picks a person who looks like they're dreaming off about something else.

I turned my mind back to class—just in time for a question.

"Who knows who the Surgeon General *is?*" Ms. Cramm asked.

Andrea's hand went up. It's incredible how Andrea can keep on being so popular even when her hand is always up with an answer in almost every class. Except math. She's real stupid in math.

Ms. Cramm called on her, and Andrea said, "I guess the Surgeon General is the chief doctor of the United States, the way the Attorney General is the chief lawyer of the United States."

"Well," said Ms. Cramm, "that's more or less the idea."

"And," said Rodney Fiedler, "he's been sticking all these slogans on the cigarette packs. 'The Surgeon General warns that cigarette smoking is dangerous to your health.'"

"Yes," said Ms. Cramm, "it's a government ruling. Since 1976 that warning has had to go on every single pack of cigarettes."

"Not that anyone pays any attention to it!" said Pete.

I looked at him. I guess I like him in a kind of way. Not as a *boy* or anything. Just as a person. I wondered if I could invite him to my party. If Roger came, I'd have to invite some other boy so Roger wouldn't feel too stupid being there with six or seven girls.

"You're wrong about that, Peter," said Ms. Cramm. "This book"—and she held it up again, high, like a weight for muscle building—"this is the Surgeon General's second report on cigarette smoking. It was published in 1979. The Surgeon General's *first* report came out in 1964. It was a much thinner book. With far fewer findings. But still very scary. And in the years between the two reports cigarette smoking among adults has dropped sharply. And among *doctors*—twenty years ago seventy per cent of them smoked cigarettes. Now, about seven per cent do. In fact, *everyone* is smoking less. Even teen-agers."

She put the volume on the science library shelf. "If you want to learn more about what *kinds* of trouble cigarette smoking can cause, you can come up after class and look at this book."

Sandy Weatherall gave another sigh, a louder one. A sigh of relief. The cigarette-smoking-pollution part of the period was over!

I felt relieved too. I could just mention to my Mom about the thirty thousand research papers all proving that cigarette smoking was bad for you. If I didn't know what was *in* the papers, I wouldn't have to go on about it.

But even though Ms. Cramm put the book back on the shelf, it turned out that she still had something to say on the subject.

"Remember, it took over fifty years for medical evidence on human beings to be established in such a clear manner that the Surgeon General could issue his official government warning. But how many millions of men and women have died in the world during those fifty years because of lung cancer and heart disease and other ailments caused or complicated by cigarette smoking?"

This was one of those think-about-it questions that she didn't expect anyone to raise their hands for. And no one did.

But she answered it herself in a way. "Based on past statistics, the Surgeon General said that this year alone, cigarettes would *kill* three hundred and forty-six thousand Americans. After that cheery announcement, Ms. Cramm said, "Lights, please, Rodney." (Rodney always sits in the seat next to the light switch in science class. Maybe, since he's very little for a boy—even for a girl—it makes him feel big, plunging us all into darkness with the flick of his finger. And lighting us all up again.)

"Shades, please," Ms. Cramm said.

The kids sitting near the windows pulled the shades down. And Ms. Cramm pulled down the big white screen so that it hung in front of the blackboard. Then she walked to the back of the room where her slide projector always sits on the ready.

I groaned inside. And Sandy Weatherall groaned outside. About the last thing he or I were longing to see right now was a slide that showed somebody's disgusting smoke-polluted lung.

But instead of this what we saw on the screen was a handsome gray-haired doctor wearing a white coat. And guess what he was holding up? A pack of cigarettes. And guess what he was saying? In big black print. "Cigarette smoking is beneficial to your health." And in smaller print—which I could read only by squinting my eyes—it said how cigarette smoking made you relaxed and was good for your blood pressure and all.

"This," said Ms. Cramm, "is a slide made from an

advertisement run by a cigarette company forty years ago. There were actually ad campaigns saying that cigarettes were *good* for you."

"But that guy's a doctor," Sandy Weatherall said loudly. "He should know."

"A white coat does not a doctor make," said Ms. Cramm. "Any model can put on a doctor's white coat. The ad doesn't *say* he's a doctor, does it?"

That shut Sandy Weatherall up.

Ms. Cramm clicked on to another slide. This was a blow-up of a newspaper story. The headline read, "Cigarette Companies Offer Scientific Proof; Smoking is Harmless." I tried to squint-read what the rest of the story said. But I couldn't make it out. Then Ms. Cramm said, "Lights, Rodney," and when he flicked the switch, she walked back to the front of the room.

She sat on her desk, and leaned forward a little— like she does when she wants to make very sure we get the idea. As if she's a human exclamation point.

"That second kind of ad campaign was started up by the cigarette companies about *twenty* years ago. What do you think made them change their tune?"

Some hands went up. But this time it was a spring-upon question. "Sandy?" she said.

Sandy said, "Huh?"

Ms. Cramm repeated patiently, "First cigarette companies said smoking was beneficial. Then, in the early sixties they announced that *their* scientific studies showed smoking was harmless to the health. As a matter of fact, some of the companies are *still* saying that. Now, Sandy, why do you think they changed their message from beneficial to harmless?"

Sandy shrugged. So she called on Doris Oberbeck.

"Well," said Doris, "maybe scientists were starting to give in reports saying that cigarettes weren't so hot for you. So the companies couldn't go on saying cigarettes were *good* for you. But they at least had to make people think cigarettes weren't bad for you. Otherwise, everyone might have stopped smoking. And the companies would have gone broke."

"That's about it, Doris," Ms. Cramm said. "Now, here's another question. The research scientists did most of their early studies on rats and mice and monkeys. Not on human beings. Why? Jody?"

I was ready for her spring in that I was listening hard. But I wasn't sure of the answer. "Well—" I said, "maybe because they didn't think it would be nice to experiment on humans. I mean, giving them cancer and all."

People laughed. Or sort of snickered. I did too. It was a stupid answer.

But Ms. Cramm put an end to the snickering when she said, "You're right, Jody. And there's another reason that follows right along with that."

She waited. It was like a blackboard eraser had wiped over my mind. That happens sometimes when a teacher calls on me. Even if I know the answer, it's wiped out. Then Pete waved his hand, and she called on him.

"Animals die young," he said. "What I mean is, they die sooner than humans usually. So you don't have to wait around so long to see if they come down with cancer and stuff."

"Exactly," said Ms. Cramm. "That's why most scientific studies on disease start with animal experimentation. Also, of course, we can cut up animals to study their cells under the microscope. Obviously, that's a lot easier to do with animals than with humans. And the early studies on animals *did* show that cigarette smoking could cause cancer and other killer diseases. But what do you think most smokers said about these early studies? Rodney?"

"Lights?" Rodney jumped up.

"No, not yet," said Ms. Cramm. And she answered the question herself. "They said, 'I'm not a mouse or a monkey. So these findings don't apply to *me.*' And they kept right on smoking. Meanwhile the cigarette companies kept coming up with *their* findings, proving —*they* said—that smoking was harmless, harmless, harmless."

"They *tricked* the people!" Pete said, with anger.

"Well," said Ms. Cramm, "you can't blame it all on the cigarette companies. The scientists gave the warnings. If people had listened—if they'd cut out smoking then—hundreds of thousands of people who have died from lung cancer, for example, would be alive right now."

Sandy raised his hand. "Maybe they would have got lung cancer even if they didn't smoke cigarettes."

"That's a sound scientific response, Sandy," Ms. Cramm said. "But an interesting fact is this. Notice, I said *fact*. Forty years ago lung cancer was almost unknown among women. Men had been smoking for centuries. But not women. And then, around the 1930s, the tobacco companies realized they could double their market if they got women to smoke too. So they put on all these attractive ad campaigns aimed at women. If you ever see old 1930s movies on TV, notice how the women keep lighting up cigarettes.

Strange coincidence—but at that time, tobacco companies gave a lot of money to people who wanted to make movies. And their payoff was all these lady movie stars glamorously exhaling cigarette smoke. Of course, the ad campaign went on in magazines and newspapers and radio too. No TV in those days. And the campaign worked. Cigarette smoking became a very 'in' thing for women. And today—forty years later—lung cancer, which once was almost unknown among women, is now common. At least, among women who smoke."

A stiff silence spread through the classroom. I guess each person was thinking of someone they knew who smoked a lot. Someone they knew and loved.

"Here's one over-all figure in the Surgeon General's report," said Ms. Cramm. She took an index card from the desk, and read us a sentence. "Cigarette smokers have about a seventy per cent greater chance of dying from disease than nonsmokers."

Why was Ms. Cramm laying all this heavy stuff on us? It was a lot better when we were studying amoebas. After all, who cares what happens to an *amoeba*?

Then she told us why she was telling us. "For *two* reasons," she said. "Number one, since it's been proved beyond a shadow of a doubt that cigarette smoking is harmful to your health, how about making a little history? Why not become the first class in this school to try a turnaround? *Why not make it cool NOT to smoke cigarettes?*"

Nobody answered. Maybe because we were all wondering what the second reason was. I sure was wondering anyway.

Ms. Cramm slid down from the desk. (She's short and her shoes are about a foot from the floor when she's sitting on the desk. So she always lands with a slight thump.) "The second reason I've told you all this is one I don't think any of you will guess. And if, by chance, you *do* guess, you may not want to hear about it."

This time the silence was filled with uneasiness and unasked questions. What could it *be* that we didn't know and wouldn't want to know if we did know it?

7

Ms. Cramm kept us hanging there in suspense.

That's part of the way she teaches. She sometimes uses stillness to gather in everyone's attention. It's strange, if the teacher is talking, your mind will sometimes wander far off. But if the talking suddenly stops and she stands still and is silent, your attention zooms in as though she's a magnet.

She kept up the silence until even the kids who'd been whispering in the back row were staring at her, waiting. Then when the wall clock made its loud click onto the next minute, she told us.

"The research on *pot* smoking," she said, "is about at the same stage that research on tobacco smoking was ten years ago. Scientists—from many countries—are coming up with some scary findings about marijuana. Many of these findings show that marijuana is even *worse* for human beings than tobacco."

"How could that be?" said Roger loudly.

Everyone looked at him surprised, since Roger never says anything in any class. He's very handsome and he seems to think he should get good marks just for *that*.

"I mean—" said Roger, "everyone *knows* that pot is harmless!"

"Sure," said Ms. Cramm. "Harmless. Harmless. Harmless. Just what they used to say about cigarettes!"

Roger frowned. He shrugged. He kind of slunk down into his seat. I knew why he didn't want to hear anything bad about pot. He not only smokes it, he deals. Probably if he came to my party, he'd buy me my birthday present out of his pot profits. I wondered if Andrea Cohen was *going* with him, or just happened to have a date with him on Saturday. I wondered if she smoked pot too. Would they toke at my party?

I hoped Roger would come to my party because I wanted Andrea to be there. But if he did come, I hoped he'd leave his grass at home. I didn't relish the idea of a bunch of stoned guests sitting around under the balloons in the dining room eating the birthday cake that Mom had made.

Suddenly it struck me that if I invited *Pete*, it would balance out Roger. I could even imagine Pete saying it was cool *not* to smoke pot. He was the kind who could say that without sounding squarish. And before I hardly knew what I was doing I found myself writing an invitation in my biology notebook. I read it over.

Dear Pete: I'm having a birthday party Saturday afternoon. I invited Andrea Cohen among other people. But she already has a date with Roger. She said she'd come if Roger wanted to. In case Roger asks me if any other boys are coming, I thought I'd better invite some. So if you're free and would like to come for movies and pizza followed by birthday cake and etc. at my house, please let me know by nodding your head. Sincerely, Jody.
P.S. Since I'm only asking 6 or 8 people, please keep this invitation private.

Then my problem was, how I could get the note to Pete. He was sitting two rows ahead of me. If I poked

Pruney Russell, who was right in front of me, and asked him to pass the note to Pete, Pruney would sure want to follow up and ask Pete what the note said. (By rights, Pruney should have been nicknamed Nosy! He got the name Pruney last year when he always had a box of prunes in his lunch box because he kept on being constipated. Before he got the nickname he went by his regular name, which is Willis. I guess he prefers Pruney to *that*.)

I decided the best thing to do about Pete would be to jump up as soon as the school bell sounded and biology class was over. I'd try to get my invitation into Pete's hand before he rushed out of the room. (It's strange the way everyone rushes out of one class as soon as the bell rings, and ambles slow-motion into the next class ten minutes later.)

Meanwhile, I was listening to Ms. Cramm with one ear. She'd collected a lot of material on the new research about pot. She wanted us to divide up into research teams. "We'll spend a week on the projects," she said. "You can choose which team you want to be on. Then you'll study the findings in that particular category. And each team will decide on the most effective way to present its report to the rest of the class. We'll start tomorrow. I'll be on hand to help out whenever you need me. Now, these are the areas we'll study."

Everyone was quiet as her chalk clacked along, spelling out the words:

MARIJUANA: HARMFUL EFFECTS ON:
   · Lungs and Pulmonary System
   · Reproductive System: Male and Female
   · Brain

- Cells and Chromosomes
- Driving Ability
- Psychological

"I'm taking reproduction," Sandy Weatherall whispered to me. "You want to be on my team?"

"Well—" I stalled. I felt I should take Lungs and Pulmonary for the reason that my sister has this little dry cough she keeps coughing all the time. She even told me it's a pot cough. Like you might say you've got a broken-off fingernail and so what? But supposing the research showed her that cough might turn into something more than "so what"?

"Reproduction," Sandy said. "That translates into S-E-X."

"Yeah," I told him. "Well, I'll have to see which topic sounds the best."

I would have felt flattered that Sandy wanted me on his research team except for the fact that he's like a male Francene. Popularity-wise, I mean. He's sort of a nerd. He's got this reddish hair which is spiky at the ends. Maybe that's from oiliness because he doesn't wash it very much. And he always smells a little like the boys' gym after a basketball game. Even though he, himself, isn't much of an athlete. In fact, he tries his best to get out of gym and basketball practice. The school nurse says he's one of her best customers.

The terrible thing is that Sandy seems to like me. Why I have to be specially liked by the two biggest rejects in the whole class, I don't know.

Then Roger spoke up again. "What about the other side?"

Ms. Cramm looked at him. "What do you mean exactly, Roger?"

"You should have a research topic about all the reports that pot is harmless. That's what I mean," said Roger. "My brother showed me these reports. There's plenty of them."

"Okay," said Ms. Cramm, "we can have a research topic called the Other Side." And she wrote this below Psychological on the blackboard. "However"— she turned and looked straight at Roger—"since this is a research project—and a science class—I'll expect the Other Siders to tell us *when* these Other Side studies were published. Most of them were based on research done before 1972. Before sophisticated scientific methods were developed to study the effects of marijuana."

Roger raised his hand. "I volunteer to be the chairman of the Other Side."

But Ms. Cramm told him that no one could volunteer for any research team until she had given us a little information about each of the subjects on the blackboard. "Since we don't have much time left this period, and since a picture is worth a thousand words, I'll start by showing you a few slides. Rodney, lights please. Shades, please."

For one short moment there was complete darkness. Everyone started talking in low voices. Pot was something we were all interested in. A few, like Roger, were already smoking and dealing. Some were smoking whenever they could get some. A lot had tried it. And there were some, like me, who hadn't tried yet but who would soon. Because there was someone always wanting to sell us a joint or a nickel bag (five dollars worth) .

I took advantage of the darkness and the murmur

of talking to stand up, lean over Pruney, and tap Pete on the shoulder. "Here," I whispered. "A note for you." And I sat down quick. Just as the room became lit a little by the light from the slide projector.

Then there came onto the screen a picture of two blobs. One was nice and round. The other was smaller and its edges were all sort of crumpling in.

"These are white blood cells," said Ms. Cramm. "They look entirely different. But in fact they are exactly the same *type* of cell. The only difference is that one comes from a forty-year-old man who's been smoking cannabis since he was sixteen. The other comes from a forty-year-old man in the same village who has never smoked cannabis."

"What's cannabis?" asked Pruney.

"You'll be reading a lot about it in your material," said Ms. Cramm. "It's the Latin name of the plant from which marijuana and hashish are prepared."

"What's hashish?" asked Doris Oberbeck.

I was glad she'd asked because I didn't know myself —though I'd heard of it. Suddenly I decided to ask Doris to my party. After all, I might have to end up with her as my best friend. Which wouldn't be too bad. I didn't know her very well. But she seemed nice. And we had certain things in common. Not only did we have the smallest sets of titties in the class, but Doris didn't care yet about clothes and stuff. And certainly not about boys. She was twelve. But interestwise she was more like eleven. More like me.

When I came back to attention, Roger was talking about the difference between pot and hashish. "With hash," he said, "the THC content is higher and so is the price. You can get a supply of good pot for—"

"This is a biology class," said Ms. Cramm sharply. "We don't need to go into the economics. And as far as comparing the THC content—"

"What's THC?" asked Doris. "It sounds like mouthwash."

"That's TCP," said Ms. Cramm. "THC is one of the psychoactive—or mind-altering—parts of cannabis. In Europe, people tend to smoke hashish more than pot. This study was made in a village in Greece. And the THC content of the hashish smoked by men in that village is four to five per cent."

"How much THC is there in pot?" asked Doris Oberbeck. I wondered why she was so interested in all this. Maybe she was a secret smoker and I *shouldn't* have her as my understudy choice for best friend.

"Well," said Ms. Cramm, "what the pot dealers call 'good stuff' can have a THC content around four or five per cent. Some of it's over six per cent. So, what's the warning that *this* slide gives?" She answered the question herself. "Kids who are starting to smoke pot now risk cell damage if they keep up the smoking for twenty or thirty years."

All this didn't mean too much to me. Like Ms. Cramm had said before, in kids' terms twenty or thirty years is the same as Forever. Or Never. Besides, it's hard to relate to a cell.

"The research team working on Cells and Chromosomes," said Ms. Cramm, "will learn exactly what these abnormal cells can mean in terms of your own health. For instance, since certain white blood cells fight disease germs, pot—some scientists say—can weaken the immune system. So the pot smoker will eventually get sick more and stay sick longer than the non-pot smoker."

Then she switched to the next slide.

On one side of the screen was something that looked like a fat, dark gourd or turnip. On the other side was an ikky-looking, strung-out shape, all spotty.

"This," said Ms. Cramm "is from the same study of long-time hashish smokers. The plump dark cell is a normal sperm from a man who did not smoke hashish. Though he *did* smoke tobacco. The other is a sperm from the hashish smoker."

I noticed Sandy Weatherall sitting up very straight. He was staring at the screen. I glanced around the room. Most of the boys were sitting up straight, and staring. But Roger wasn't. He was slumped down in his seat, like he was too bored to listen to any of this.

Then I noticed that Peter wasn't looking at the screen. He was looking at me. And he was moving his lips to say something, but without any sound coming out. If I was a deaf person and could read lips it would have been okay. But as it was I didn't have the foggiest idea what he was saying. One thing was sure. He wasn't nodding—which is what my note had said he should do, if he could come to my party.

Since I couldn't comprehend him, I just shrugged. A great big shrug, so he could be sure to see it in the feeble light from the slide projector.

Then Pete motioned to the front door. I guess he was saying that we'd meet in the hall after class and he'd explain.

I nodded, okay.

My hope sank, however. If he *could* come, all it

took was a nod from him. I even felt kind of a fool now for inviting him. I mean, even though I did sort of like him we didn't have any relationship except to "Hi" each other when we passed in the hall. He probably thought it was weird of me to invite him—practically a stranger—to my *birthday* party. At least, thank goodness, I'd explained about Roger in my note, which made it sound a little more logical.

Another slide! Two more cells, which, it turned out, were sections of lungs from a rat. One of the sections had a lot of little strands running through it. The other looked more empty. I wondered which was the good one.

"In this study," said Ms. Cramm, "rats inhaled marijuana smoke at the human equivalent of one to two joints a day for six months."

A few people giggled.

"Something funny?" Ms. Cramm asked.

"Do you have a slide of a rat smoking a joint and getting stoned?" said Roger.

"Okay," said Ms. Cramm. "That's a valid question. How does a scientist get marijuana smoke into an animal? In this experiment, the rat was placed in a small plastic container. The container was attached to a puffing machine. All that the rats got was a carefully regulated two or three puffs of smoke. Which equals about one joint for a human. With a mouse, a fraction of a puff equals one human joint. So don't be thrown off by people who tell you, 'Naturally, you give a mouse a big enough dose of anything and he'll come down with cancer, or he'll die.' The important point is that in the new findings on marijuana, animals have been given very *small* doses."

"Which rat in those slides has the best lungs?" asked Andrea Cohen.

"The one on the left," said Ms. Cramm. "All these little lines are air passageways. That rat can breath nicely, normally. In the slide on the right, a lot of the deeper air passageways have just—disappeared. This can lead to a serious condition. In the last stages, after some years, there can be complete lung failure."

I felt a little chill go through me. Were Linda's air passageways *disappearing*? I don't usually call out without being called on. But this time I did. "How much pot did they get in human terms? How many joints a day?"

"The rats," said Ms. Cramm slowly, "were given puffs of smoke with THC every day for six months—which equals ten to fifteen years in a human life. The few puffs they got were the *human* equivalent of one to two joints a day." Then she added, "A lot of the older kids in this school smoke more than that."

Linda did. Sometimes she smoked a joint when we waited for the school bus in the morning. She liked to get to school stoned. That way, she said, school wasn't such a drag. She smoked in the park during her free periods, and after school. And she usually smokes at least one joint after dinner when she lies back on her pillows and plays records. Pot gets her more into her music, she says.

"As far as human studies go," Ms. Cramm said, "a lung specialist at the UCLA School of Medicine did studies which show that if a person smokes one joint a day, he—or she—would get airflow obstruction which would *not* develop if a person smoked sixteen tobacco cigarettes a day."

I decided definitely to be on the Lung and Pulmonary Research Team. Sometimes I hate my sister. Especially lately, she's turned quite obnoxious. But even so, I wouldn't want her little pot cough leading into complete lung failure in twenty years.

"Lights, Rodney. Shades, please," Ms. Cramm said. And as the room sprang into brightness, she walked to her desk.

"I don't have time this period to show you brain cells of rhesus monkeys. Potted cells, you might call them—of monkeys given the human equivalent of one 'street joint' three times a day, five days a week. For six months. This would equal two to three years in a human being."

Two to three years. That's about how long Linda had been smoking grass! I listened hard.

"The brain cells from the pot-smoked monkeys were compared to the same kind of brain cells from monkeys who had *no* THC in the smoke they were given. Tomorrow I'll show you the slides. You can see the differences very clearly. And because it's the *brain*—I find these slides the scariest of all."

She checked off the first four subjects on the blackboard. "As for marijuana's effect on driving—those of you who chose this subject will find that pot has just as bad effects on driving as alcohol does."

"And for those of you interested in the psychological effects—one of them is the so-called dropout syndrome. This doesn't mean that pot smokers necessarily drop out of school. But they often drop out of *caring* about school. Their grades go down. They give up things they once were interested in. And the more they smoke, the more they drop out of everything. Except the life that revolves around pot. Many become irritable. And sometimes their behavior is quite irrational—though it seems just fine to them."

God! She was describing Linda! Could *pot* have changed my sister from the really nice person she used to be—into her today's self?

I decided to ask Ms. Cramm about this after class.

The school bell rang.

I started up toward the teacher's desk.

And then I remembered Pete.

I hurried out into the hallway.

8

Pete was right there, waiting for me.

I thought again how nice it must be to have someone who would wait for you after class. Just to be with you for a few minutes till the next period. Like Linda and Steve.

Except in the case of Pete, I knew he was only waiting to tell me why he couldn't come to my party.

"Thanks a lot for inviting me," Pete said.

I sort of shrugged.

"I'd like to come," Pete said.

I waited for the But.

"But I was supposed to go downtown with my mother on Saturday afternoon. I have a dentist appointment and then she was going to take me to get my eyes tested."

"Oh," I said, "will you have to wear glasses?"

"I can't see the blackboard too well," Pete said. "Unless I squint."

"I can't either unless I squint," I said.

He looked at me and smiled, as though we had something really great in common. "Maybe you should get your eyes tested too," he said.

I nodded. "Well," I said, "I'm real sorry you can't come to my party."

"I didn't say I couldn't come," Pete said. "I just wanted to explain why I might not be able to. I'm going to ask my mother if she can change the dentist appointment till the next Saturday."

"Oh," I said, flattered that he would even think

about going to all that trouble. "And what about the eyeglasses appointment?"

"We don't have an appointment," Pete said. "It's one of those places where you just stop in and wait."

"Oh," I said.

"So, I'll let you know," Pete said, and he walked away.

I glanced back into the classroom. Ms. Cramm was still at her desk. She was talking to Roger and some other kids. I wanted to wait till she was alone so I could ask her a couple of questions in private.

Then Corinne came down the hall. Even though we're in the same grade, we don't have too many classes together. In fact, she has a lot of classes with Kim. And she was with Kim now. They were laughing about something.

Corinne saw me. I looked away quickly.

Suddenly Corinne was next to me. And Kim was walking into the math classroom.

"What's the matter with you?" Corinne said.

"What do you mean, what's the matter?" I said.

"You can't even say hi to me?"

"Oh," I said. "I thought you were otherwise occupied. You seemed to be very busy with Kim."

"What—I can't talk to anybody except you, without you getting all mad about it?"

"No. I didn't say that," I said. My voice came out cramped-sounding.

"I don't know what's got into you these last couple of days," Corinne said. "You've been so obnoxious."

"Well," I said, "thanks a lot!"

"Look," Corinne said. "Obviously, I'm not getting through to you. Everything I say is wrong. And since

I don't know what's gotten into you, there's no use of me trying to pry it out of you. So I'm just going to leave you alone. If you feel like coming around, then come around."

And she walked off and went into the math classroom.

Naturally, that left me feeling just great.

Probably she wouldn't even come to my party.

It would be a birthday party with one guest. Reject Francene.

Doris Oberbeck passed me. And in a kind of desperation, and so I wouldn't have to think about the hurt in me caused by Corinne, I ran after Doris. "Hey," I said, "wait up."

Doris waited up.

"Are you busy on Saturday afternoon?" I asked. No use in laying out the whole invitation business, if she couldn't come in the first place.

"Why do you ask?" Doris Oberbeck said.

Whatever made me think I'd want such a snot for my understudy best friend?

"Well—" I said, "I wasn't planning to have a birthday party. But I suddenly decided to have one. My birthday's on Saturday. Movies, pizza parlor, and stuff. I'd like you to come if you can come."

"I can come," said Doris.

I looked at her, feeling a little stunned. And right away I liked her again. Nice and simple and straight. *I can come.* Just the very three simple words to make me feel a little better.

Then guess who comes sailing up? Francene! "I meant to ask you, Jody," she said. "What are you wearing to your party? I mean, is it a blue-jeans kind of party? Or should I wear a skirt, or what?"

Oh, god, I thought to myself. Probably when Doris finds who's the only other one on the guest list so far, she'll remember something else she had to do on Saturday afternoon.

Francene was plumped there, waiting for an answer.

"I'm wearing blue jeans," I said.

"Good," said Doris Oberbeck.

"Oh, you coming too?" said Francene.

"Listen, Francene," I said, "I'm only inviting a few people. I mean, about eight. So please don't go blabbing about it all over. What if I *hadn't* invited Doris —and she's standing right here listening. She would have been insulted."

"I'm—sorry," said Francene. And she looked very sorry. "I didn't think."

"That's okay," I said.

"I think that's very nice of you to be so considerate about people's feelings," Francene said. "It *is* insulting to people when they hear there's a party and they're not invited. See you, Jody. See you, Doris." And she walked on down the hall.

"Who else are you having?" Doris asked. It was an understandable question. I mean, I don't know anybody who ever invited Francene to their party.

"Well—" I said, "Corinne. Probably. And Andrea Cohen. If Roger can come. She has a date with him that day. And Pete if he can get out of going to the dentist. And some others I haven't asked yet."

"Sounds good," said Doris. "Thanks for asking me." And she went on into math class.

I went back into the science room. Everyone had gone now, except Roger and Ms. Cramm.

"You'll have to remember," Ms. Cramm was saying, "there's another side to the Other Side."

Roger looked at her kind of blankly.

"What I mean," said Ms. Cramm, "in your Other Side report, you'll probably mention glaucoma. Right?"

"Right!" said Roger. "Pot is good for your eyes."

"It is not good for your eyes," said Ms. Cramm. "It may help one of the symptoms for one eye disease. Glaucoma. But the help lasts only for two hours. If you were going to use pot as a treatment you'd have to smoke a joint every two hours, night and day."

Roger had kind of a loopy grin, as though this would be the greatest medicine he could think of.

"However," said Ms. Cramm, "in your Other Side report, I'll expect you to mention, for example, that the director of the International Glaucoma Congress —a very important eye doctor—says that pot is definitely not a good treatment. The best way to treat glaucoma is with special eye drops, which we have. And these eye drops have no bad side effects, which pot *can* have."

"Well," said Roger, "I don't know too much about how it cures eyes. But I do know pot cures cancer."

"Oh," said Ms. Cramm, as though he had hurt her. "Who told you that?"

"It's common knowledge," said Roger. "With people who really *know* about pot."

"Some doctors say," said Ms. Cramm, "that smoking pot helps prevent vomiting after having a chemotherapy treatment *for* cancer. And some doctors say there are better drugs to stop the vomiting. Drugs which don't have bad side effects."

Roger gave her a glowery look. I couldn't see why. I mean, so what? Even if pot does stop you upchucking when you're dying of cancer, that doesn't seem to me to be much of an Other Side.

"As a matter of fact," Ms. Cramm said, "I read about one drug company who put a lot of money into separating the element in pot which stops vomiting. They wanted to sell it as a legal prescription medicine. But when they tried it out on healthy dogs, some of the dogs died. And even if the medicine *had* worked, medicines are good for specific disease symptoms. But they can be very harmful for general use."

"I can see," said Roger, "I'm not going to get a good mark unless I come in saying that pot is rotten."

Ms. Cramm sighed. "Roger," she said, sounding very tired. "The whole point of this project is to expose students to the medical evidence about marijuana. Many kids think pot is harmless. We have the responsibility to give them some scientific facts showing that it's very harm*ful*. When I introduced the subject I said it was something you might not want to hear about. Maybe I should have said it was something pot smokers—kids and adults—wouldn't want to hear about."

"*I'm* not a pot smoker," Roger said quickly.

She nodded, like maybe she believed him and then again maybe she didn't.

"I'm talking about people you're getting your information *from*," said Ms. Cramm. "It's like a symptom, Roger. My niece—she's fifteen—summed it up in a sentence. She told me, 'I like smoking pot, Aunt Susan. And I don't want to know anything bad about it.'"

"Where does she go to school?" Roger asked.

"My niece? Cincinnati."

"Oh," said Roger.

I wondered if that had made him interested in Ms. Cramm's niece. She smoked pot.

"Did you want to see me, Jody?" Ms. Cramm said.

I nodded, and Roger walked off.

What Ms. Cramm had just told him was exactly the last thing I wanted to hear. I'd been planning to let Linda in on what I'd learn on the Lung and Pulmonary Research Team. But maybe this might turn her against me. And that was something I could do without!

"Yes, Jody?" Ms. Cramm said.

"I was wondering—will all the grades be doing this pot-research project?"

"No," said Ms. Cramm. "Not this year anyway. We thought we'd start with the seventh grade. Our assumption was that seventh graders hadn't gotten into pot yet. And we wouldn't meet the resistance we'd find from the older students."

"But why shouldn't *everyone* be told about all this new medical research?" If the school would tell Linda, I wouldn't have to get into it!

"Everyone *should* know," Ms. Cramm said. "You'll find this hard to believe, Jody—but I had a very tough time persuading the powers that be to let me use one week of my seventh-grade biology semester for these pot-research projects."

"*Why?*" I did find it hard to believe.

"It's a very strange business," Ms. Cramm said. "And please don't quote me on this. But the fact is that kids aren't the only ones who turn off when you present evidence that pot is extremely harmful. Physically and psychologically. And kids aren't the only ones in this school who are turning on."

People were trying to *stop* Ms. Cramm from giving

us the information! It was scary. More scary even than the slides and the things she had said about them.

"Do you have someone who needs this information?" Ms. Cramm asked.

"Well—" I hesitated. After all, she *was* a teacher. And pot *is* illegal. So it wouldn't be so exactly nice to say that my sister is a big pot smoker.

"We hope the seventh graders will share what they learn," Ms. Cramm said. "After our own research week we can Xerox a lot of the material. You and other students can give it to people you think might— need it."

I nodded. But I couldn't see Linda sitting down and reading a lot of Xeroxed material about the bad effects of pot. More likely it would send her into fits of laughing. She'd make fun of it. And worse, she'd make fun of me.

When I left the room, I felt angry. Not at Ms. Cramm. She'd tried. But I was angry at whoever had stopped her giving this information to all the grades. Why dump all the responsibility onto the heads of the seventh graders?

As far as I could see I certainly was sensible in wanting to stay eleven. No one expects an eleven-year-old kid to teach their sixteen-year-old sister about why pot wasn't so harmless after all. Not to mention teaching their mother what all the studies on tobacco had turned up. Thirty thousand research papers proving it can kill you.

In that gloomy frame of mind, I was all set to hear the worst when Andrea Cohen ran up to me in the hall. Naturally she'd tell me Roger didn't want to come to my birthday.

But instead she said in a friendly rush of words, "It's okay, Jody. Roger says he'd like to come to your party. But he wants to know what other boys will be there."

"Well," I said, "so far I've only asked Pete. He's letting me know."

"Oh," said Andrea. "What if Pete can't come? Roger wouldn't want to be the only boy there."

I suddenly felt that whatever happened, Andrea Cohen had to be at my party. It would set a good tone to the whole thing. And it would also be of social help to me if word got out that I'd had a birthday party and Andrea Cohen had been there. "What if I asked Jimmy Angelo?" I said. Jimmy is Roger's best friend. The only trouble is, I've never spoken two words to Jimmy.

Andrea said, "That would be great. Let me know."

Then the bell rang for the next class. And Andrea ran down the hall to math and I ran up the stairs to French.

While Mademoiselle Blodgett was writing some irregular verbs on the blackboard, I made out my guest list. In fact, I made out two lists. One looked very satisfactory. *Andrea. Corinne. Pete. Doris. Jimmy. Roger. Francene. Jody.* Eight was a good number. The other list looked awful. *Doris. Jody. Francene.* We three were the only sure ones. Should I ask more people in the hope that some could surely come? But what if they all showed up? Mom had said six or eight. And frankly that's all I wanted too.

"Jody," I heard Mademoiselle Blodgett say.

"*Oui, mademoiselle?*"

She repeated the question, which was how do you

say, "Are we going to Monsieur Duval's house tonight?"

Maybe I would have known how to say it if I'd had
time to think it out. But with all my other problems I
somehow couldn't think straight about going to Monsieur Duval's. I stammered around and Mademoiselle
Blodgett gave me a dirty look—which can look especially dirty in French. And she called on someone else
for the answer.

Actually, Mademoiselle Blodgett's looks shouldn't
be any dirtier than anyone else's, since she's not even
French. She comes from Grand Rapids, Minnesota.
And she always puts the accent on the Grand. She
taught at Itasca Community College there. And when
she tells us that she always puts the accent on College. She says we have to call her Mademoiselle since
she's the French teacher. But from the sound of the
French cassettes we listen to for pronunciation, Mademoiselle Blodgett is speaking another language entirely.

After French, I rushed down the stairs and waited
outside the math-class door. I know that Jimmy is in
Corinne's math class because she told me how he likes
to sit next to her when they have a test. He's tall for
his age and he cranes his long neck when the teacher
isn't looking, so he can see what Corinne has as answers. (She happens to be an A math student.) Sometimes she has to cup her hand around her answers to
keep him from cheating.

Jimmy came out of the room, talking to a couple of
other kids. Since I felt the whole success of my guest
list depended on him, I clutched hold of his shirt in
front and sort of pulled him off, away from the
others.

Naturally, he looked at me kind of surprised.

"I know I hardly know you," I said quickly. "But—" And I explained about Andrea Cohen and Roger and my birthday party. "Since you're Roger's best friend," I said, "Andrea told me to ask you too."

"What movie are you going to see?" Jimmy asked.

"Well—I don't know. Whatever's on at the Riviera we'll see."

"Maybe it's something I've already seen," said Jimmy.

"But they change movies every Saturday. And my party's on Saturday."

"Sometimes I go over to Clintonville to see a movie," Jimmy said. "The Riviera often gets the same film I already saw at the Clintonville Bijoux."

"Well," I said, "I'll find out what's playing at the Riviera and I'll let you know."

"Don't bother," said Jimmy.

My spirits sank. There went the good guest list.

But he hadn't meant it that way at all. "If I've seen the movie and I don't want to see it again, I'll come afterwards for the eating."

"Oh, that's great!" I said. I felt like giving him a kiss. Not that kind of kiss. Just out of gratitude.

Suddenly the good guest list headed by Andrea Cohen had come through.

Maybe this was a good omen and *everything* would turn out right from this moment on.

And, in fact, things did go pretty well all the rest of that day. Until around eight o'clock that night. Then is when the worst time of my life began.

9

When I got home from school, guess what? There was Linda standing in front of the bathroom mirror plucking her eyebrows—in my blue blouse.

First I felt angry. I mean, it was Friday that she said she wanted it for. And this was only Thursday. Then Linda turned to me with such a sweet put-on smile. "I just tried it on to see what skirt I'd wear it with," she said. "I love this blouse."

"Well, keep it," I said.

"Reeealy?" said Linda. "You mean it?"

I shrugged. "It fits you. It doesn't fit me yet."

"But you'll grow into it," Linda said.

By that time, if she liked it this much, she'd have borrowed it so much it would feel like a hand-me-down from her. Probably I'd get the most out of the blouse by using it to get her nice to me. It would be helpful having her nice at my birthday party.

"I *want* you to have it," I said.

"Wow," said Linda. "Thanks!" Then she turned from the mirror and smiled. "I think I'll give you your present tonight," she said.

"Why not wait till my birthday?"

"Because this is something you might want to use for your birthday. So it's better to get it ahead."

I felt excited-puzzled. I mean, as far as I could see the only good thing about having a twelve-year-old birthday was the presents. Dad's had been okay. Though they were better in their gift wrap than when I opened them. Mom's obviously wouldn't be much.

But Linda's might be the really big something that would make this birthday really good.

To sort of test out her good will I said, "Do you want to help me put up balloons for my party?"

"Sure," said Linda. "Why don't we do it right now?"

"Two days ahead?"

"Well," she said, "Steve and I are going out tomorrow night. Do it now, that's my motto."

Do it *now*? I'll do it later. I'll do it tomorrow. I'll do it next week. That's what she mostly said about things. But if she wanted to do it now, that was fine with me.

Mom had bought some balloons in the supermarket and Linda and I went down to the Dining Room and started blowing. Balloons are great. The whole box only cost $1.59. I don't know any other thing that can turn a regular room into something special for $1.59.

And we had fun blowing. Linda wasn't too hot at it. She had trouble getting them started. And then when they did swell up with air, sometimes she'd keep on blowing till the balloon burst in her face. Then we'd laugh together. It's the first time we'd laughed together for a long time. We brought up the step ladder from the cellar, and tied the balloons to the light fixtures and the venetian blinds and Scotch-taped some to the walls. They made the room look really great.

"I remember my twelve-year-old birthday party," Linda said. "Dad and I put up the balloons and we had these crepe-paper runners looping around between the balloons. And we laughed so much."

I felt a sharp pang of jealousy. At *her* twelfth birthday she'd had a whole family. Diane hadn't been hired yet as Dad's bookkeeper. And maybe Mom and Dad hadn't even started their fighting. Maybe if I had a complete family like that I wouldn't be so scared about being twelve.

After a while Mom came home. And that turned into something good too. She was excited about her date—even though she pretended not to be.

She called us into her room to help her decide what to wear. I chose a chiffon sort of dress. It was old. Back from the Dad-days. But I liked it. "It makes you look nice and floaty, Mom," I said.

"Spacy is the word," said Linda.

"And fat is the other word," said Mom. She put my choice back in the closet.

"Try *this* one, Mom," Linda said. And she took out a clingy kind of navy dress. "Sexeee!" said Linda, as Mom pulled the dress over her head.

Mom looked at herself in the long closet mirror. For a moment I saw a reflected sadness on her mirror face. "The last time I wore this dress . . ." she said. And that's all she said. I guess she was thinking of a time when we were a whole family. Then she sort of shook her head; shaking the memory off maybe. "Don't you think *this* makes me look fat?" She was asking Linda.

"It makes you look great, Mom," Linda said. "Like a woman—not a real estate lady. *Or* a mother. Now sit down and let me give you a new hair-do."

I watched them, feeling out of it. Linda took the barrette from Mom's hair and brushed it loose. It did look better that way. And she got her own mascara and eye liner and put it on Mom. The two of them were laughing together, and close. The closer they got, the more apart I felt. My Mama was my only real security. And Linda was sort of taking her away from me. I minded a lot. On the other hand, this was much better than the usual way, with Linda very disagreeable and complaining how Mom was hassling her.

"What's he like?" Linda asked as she put some cream rouge on Mom's cheeks.

"Well," said Mom, "I don't really know. I always thought he was awfully nice. But when a man is somebody else's husband you don't give him too much thought—that way. So I know him. But I don't know him. If you know what I mean." Mom laughed. And Linda did too. She gave Mom a little hug around the shoulders.

I just stood there like I wasn't even in the room. I felt jealous. And uneasy at seeing Mama becoming somebody else. On the other hand, the sound of laughing was very good. First it had been me laughing with Linda. And now Linda laughing with Mom.

Suddenly I remembered all the gloomy things I'd learned from Ms. Cramm. But those things could wait. After I was twelve I'd tell Mom about the thirty thousand research papers on cigarettes. And I'd tell Linda about what pot does to the lungs. Maybe I'd ask her to hear me rehearse my Lung and Pulmonary research report. Before I gave it to the class. That way Linda could hear the new news about pot. Without me having to tell her.

But I sure wasn't going to spoil my last two days of

being eleven by coming on with all this heavy stuff now.

When Linda had finished making up Mom, she stood back and looked—like an artist examining her creation. "Very good," she said. "We could pass for sisters."

"Not quite!" Mom said. But she seemed pleased.

I had to admire Linda. She herself usually dresses like a slob. But she knows how to look good if she wants to. And now she had made Mom look good too.

"Well," I said, "I have to go do some homework."

It's not so often in our house that such a happy scene happens. I sort of didn't know how to take it. So I left.

Around seven o'clock the doorbell rang. My heart started beating hard. If mine did, I can imagine how Mom's was going.

Maybe he'd be my new Dad. Then, instead of having almost no Dads, I'd have two Dads. While I was busy daydreaming this, Mom called. And I went downstairs, hoping hard that I'd like him and he'd like me and most of all that he'd like Mom.

He looked like a Clive Anderson.

In case you're not clear what a Clive Anderson looks like, he had gray hair. And he was tall, with broad shoulders. And very nice-looking. For someone that age, I mean. I guess he was in his late fifties. Mom's in her early forties. That would match up okay, I guess.

He held out his hand to shake with me. "So you must be—uh—"

"Jody," I said.

"Yes. Your mother's told me all about you. I hear you're having a birthday, young lady."

I nodded.

"Twelve years old," he said. "I have a daughter who's just turned twelve."

"You *do*?" I suddenly envisioned her living here with us. We'd get twin beds in my room and she'd live here with me. We'd share the room. Share everything. I'd always have someone to talk to. "Where is she? Your daughter?"

"She's with her mother. In Rhode Island," Clive Anderson said.

I nodded. And sat down on the couch. It was the same couch I'd sat on yesterday with my Dad. Maybe I'd soon be thinking of him as my other Dad. Probably Clive Anderson would like me better than Linda. Because I'd remind him of his own daughter living far away in Rhode Island.

Just then Linda came into the room. And Clive Anderson stood up. "Well," he said, "here's another beauty."

I wondered who he had meant as the first beauty. Mom? Or me? Since I'm not much of a beauty, I guess he meant Mom. Although she's not too much of a beauty either. Linda got all the luck in that department.

When Mom and Clive Anderson went out the door together I said to Linda, "I wonder if they'll get married."

Linda stared at me. "You wonder WHAT?"

"Well," I said, feeling real dumb, "Mom *likes* him."

"Look," said Linda, "it's the first time she's been out with him. Or anyone. For months. What she likes is the idea of going out. With a nice-looking man."

"Well, everything has to begin somewhere," I said, trying to sound wise.

"True," said Linda. "But there are a lot of things that 'everything' can mean, apart from marriage."

I nodded. Then I started upstairs. Linda came after me. She went into her room. And I went into her room too. It was nice the way we were talking together. And I wanted to keep on with it. But Linda said, "Could you go?"

I looked at her.

"Are you insulted?" Linda said.

I said, "No."

"Are you sure you're not insulted? I have to do my homework. Maybe we can watch TV together later."

"Okay," I said. And I left.

Maybe she wanted to get stoned or something. Or talk to Steve on the telephone. She has no phone in her room. But she has a jack. And when she's done with her homework (or *says* she's done with it) Mom lets her take the phone from the hall and bring it to her room. Then she plugs the phone into her jack, and she and Steve are together.

Usually I don't feel lonely in the house. Not in the nights anyway, because Mom's almost always there.

But this time I suddenly felt *hollow* with loneliness. If Linda had first been mean to me and then had told me to go, it would have been like usual. And I would have shrugged it off. But this time we were getting close. Or so I thought anyway. I was all set for a real talk about Mom and boy friends and maybe even about whether she was frustrated without any sex. It's a strange situation in the house when the Mom, who's supposed to be having it, isn't. And the sixteen-year-old daughter, who's not supposed to be having it, is. And the eleven-year-old daughter, who isn't supposed to know about what's going on behind her sister's locked door, does.

Then I heard the lock on Linda's door click closed.

I could understand her locking the door against me when she was in there with Steve. Not that I'd ever want to go in there when the two of them were making out. Even hearing the sounds from my own room is too much. But at least there's some sense then in locking the door to keep me out.

But why would she want to lock the door now, when the two of us were alone in the house?

I went back to my room and sat at my desk and opened my French book. We had a verb quiz coming up the next day. But somehow I couldn't keep my mind on conjugating the verb *avoir*.

I needed to talk to my sister real badly. And she had locked me out of her room.

10

I got through French and was on to math—formulas for rectangles and trapezoids—when I heard Linda calling me.

Right away I felt resentment. First she locks me out. Then she summons me to go down and get her a Coke and some potato chips or something. Sometimes she gets the munchies when she's stoned and she's afraid of running into Mom, so she orders me, like a kind of slave.

This time I decided I'd tell her to go down and get what she wanted herself. Mom wasn't home. And I was busy. So she could just move herself!

I shoved back my chair with anger, and with determination. And I walked across the hall and shoved open her door, which was now unlocked.

Then I gasped.

It wasn't Linda's room. It was some other place. There were lit candles in wine bottles. There was the murky smell of incense. And there was soft guitar music playing from the stereo. Linda had put the music on as I walked in.

"Birthday-present time!" Linda said.

I was so astonished I couldn't think of one word to say. I glanced around the room again. But there was nothing that a bicycle could be hiding behind. And her closet wasn't big enough to hold a hidden bike.

Linda took a small package from behind her stereo. It was wrapped in gold paper.

With the guitar music and candlelight I sort of

knew what it was. And it wasn't what I wanted for my birthday!

"Open it!" Linda said. She sounded a lot more excited about the present than I was.

It was tied with a thin gold cord. At least the wrappings were very nice. Maybe it would be some kind of jewelry. Or perfume. Although I wasn't into those things at all yet, I hoped it was one of them. So it wouldn't be what I thought it was.

"Maybe you better sit down before you open it," Linda said. "So you don't spill anything."

"I wonder what it could be," I said, sort of stiffly.

"Here. Sit!" Linda said. And gently shoved me down on one of the fat black corduroy-covered pillows which serve, in her room, as chairs.

Linda plunked herself down next to me. "Open it carefully."

"Must be the crown jewels," I said. And I laughed a little, but it came out strangled-sounding.

I took off the gift-wrap paper. Then I took off the cover of the smooth white cardboard box. And it was what I'd thought. Everything you'd need for starting up as a pot smoker.

"Let me show you around," Linda said. It was, for me, a strange, sad sentence; a holdover from the long-ago nice times. Linda and I each used to have a dollhouse, which we made out of orange crates. What we did mostly was redecorate. We'd make furniture out of matchboxes and glue. And we'd make tiny curtains and wall-to-wall carpets from leftover material in Mom's sewing box. And sometimes we'd buy some teeny plates and irons and lamps and things from

Woolworth's. When one of us would get a room redecorated, we'd call in the other one and we'd say, "Let me show you around."

This time it was a little different. Carefully, piece by piece, Linda took little things out of the white box. First a small brass pipe. "Do you like it?" she said, real eagerly.

"Sure," I said. The word sounded like a plop. Dead.

"You know what it *is*, don't you?" said Linda.

"For pot," I said.

"I figured this was the best present I could get you," Linda said. "As a help with being twelve. You'll be able to come on real cool with the other kids in your class. By next year they'll all be smoking pot. But if you get a head start on it, they'll look up to you."

Sure, with all that we'd learned about disappearing lung passageways and sick brain cells, everyone in my class would certainly look up to me with my little pot pipe!

"A pipe is convenient," Linda said. "You can pass it around easily. And you don't have to bother with rolling papers and stuff."

I nodded.

"And this piece of plastic around the stem of the pipe is to keep your fingers cool." She looked at me. "You like it?"

"Sure," I said. "What's this other stuff?"

"These little round screens—" She picked one up. "You stick this in the bowl of the pipe, so the smoke comes through but the ashes don't."

"Oh," I said. "That's convenient."

"And this"—she held up a nice, painted wooden box—"this is a stash box. Open it."

I did. And there was this stuff like a bunch of little dried-up weeds all tangled together.

It may seem hard to believe, but I'd never even seen pot before. I could have, if I'd wanted to. But I'd always felt I wasn't ready yet. So, I'd steered clear of even looking at it.

Once I read in the paper that just over half the high school seniors in the country had tried pot. This gave me heart. In our school the pot smokers come on like everyone is doing it. But if kids told the truth in this national poll, it meant almost half *weren't* pot smokers. Not even when they got to be seniors. I'd decided I'd stick with the almost half even before I knew pot could do all these bad things to you. Then, other times, I'd decided I *would* start. It was one of the things that conflicted in me. One of the reasons I wanted to stay eleven years old.

But now, just the very day I got good reasons from Ms. Cramm as to why I shouldn't ever start, here was my sister, Linda, giving me this great ol' birthday present!

"Now I'll show you how to roll a joint," said Linda. She put some pot into her hand, then crumbled it through her fingers. This way she got out little seeds and stems. And she put these into her frisbee. What was left looked like goldish dried-out herbs. "Do you like the stash box?" she asked.

"Oh—sure," I said. "It's very pretty."

"It's hand-painted. In India. Real India-Indian. Not American Indian."

"All the way from India," I said, trying to sound impressed.

"I could have bought you one of these cutesy stash cans. A fake Coke can. Or a skateboard with a secret stash place underneath. But I figured this was more— grown-up. More appropriate."

I nodded.

"Now watch," she said. She sprinkled some pot into one of the thin white oblong papers. "I could have bought you flavored rolling papers. Grape or ba- nana or cherry. They make those special for little kids. But I thought you'd prefer the natural kind."

"Sure," I said. "Natural is always better."

"It's very important to role the joint as tight as you can." And she showed me how. Then she licked the paper along the edges. "Just wetting it with spit sticks it together. You twist it at both ends. And that's all there is to it." She held the joint out to me. "Now I'll teach you how to toke."

"What will I feel?" I said uneasily, holding the joint between my thumb and first finger.

"Well," said Linda, "everything will seem really funny. And everything will be great. So don't worry about anything."

"Will I be able to finish my homework?"

"You'll be *able* to finish it. But you—you won't want to. And your mind will wander to better things."

"Well," I said, "I have this very big history test to- morrow. Maybe I better wait." (The same history test I'd told Dad about—that I didn't have.)

"Sure, wait if you want," Linda said. "But I'm not going to wait for you because there's this show I want to watch at nine. And I want to watch stoned."

"Do you think," I asked, "I mean—is there anything about pot that's bad for you?"

Linda shrugged. "Probably it has its drawbacks. I mean, maybe it gets bad for your lungs when you're fifty years old. But I think the experiences that a person gets are much more important than worrying about your lungs at fifty. Most of the best experiences that I've ever had have been when I'm stoned."

"What kind of experiences?" I asked.

"Well—I don't know," Linda said vaguely. "It's hard to describe. Sometimes when you come down the experiences sort of disappear. But you always know you can get stoned again and have new ones."

I nodded, like I understood. But I didn't really. First of all, when I have a great experience I like to remember it. And second, I like it to come to me naturally. Not to have some drug making it happen. But naturally I didn't say any of this to Linda. I didn't want to come on as Miss Squaresy. Besides, she was being real nice. And I didn't want to turn her off so far as her niceness to me was concerned.

"In case I'm too involved by the time you're finished studying," Linda said, "I can teach you how to toke now." She got up, went to her desk, and came back with a yellow pencil. She handed it to me. "You can toke off this. Pretend it's a joint."

Since I'd read about lead poisoning, I chose the eraser end of the pencil to put in my mouth. At least someone else hadn't been sucking on this pencil already. It always seemed to me kind of icky the way one person passed a joint they'd been toking on to another person with all their germy spit on it. Sometimes the same joint gets toked by a dozen different people. I mean, you wouldn't want to brush your teeth with a toothbrush that twelve people had already used right before you. But pot smokers don't seem to consider hygiene as too important.

"Now," Linda said, "pretend to inhale. Deeply. And hold the smoke in your lungs as long as you can. That's so you get the most out of it."

"The most what?" I said.

"You'll see." Linda smiled at me, kind of dreamily.

I practiced with the pencil, drawing the air deep into my lungs and holding it there. (Meanwhile, I was remembering all those disappearing lung passageways of the rats. And probably those rats didn't even toke deeply and hold the smoke in as long as they could. I mean, why *would* they do that? They'd have more sense. I wondered if I could get by with fake toking. If I learned enough with the yellow pencil, maybe that would work. I could draw air in, hold it. And then if someone noticed that no smoke came out again, I could just say the smoke must have gotten lost in my lungs from holding it in so long.)

"The very first time you may not feel anything at all," Linda said, going on with the lesson. "You might just get a little headache or feel sleepy."

I nodded.

"On the other hand," Linda said, "this is really good stuff so you may get high the first time. I told my—contact that this was for a birthday present. He said he'd give me some specially good stuff."

"What *makes* it good?" I asked.

"The more THC, the quicker you get stoned."

At least I knew from Ms. Cramm's class what THC was. The mind-altering part of pot. I mean, if someone had asked me what I wanted for a birthday present, I don't exactly think I'd have requested to have my mind altered. As far as I'm concerned, with all the problems I've got right now I want to have all my wits about me. As my Grandma used to say. She's dead now.

Linda took a book of matches from the pocket of my blue blouse that I was now very sorry I'd given to her. And she lit up the joint she had rolled. "Since I've finished my homework," she said, "I might as well try out this special birthday good stuff. When you've finished studying for your history test, come back and join me."

"Okay," I said, and got up from the pillow. "Thanks." Inside, I felt that the thanks were for letting me go. At least for the moment. I knew I wasn't going to go back into her room to start in my career of getting stoned. I could put it off tonight by saying I wanted to have *all* my wits about me—every last one of them—for this *very* important history test tomorrow. She's told me herself that even after you come down from a high, you can't count on being all there in school the next day. So, I could make her understand about tonight. But what worried me very much was the future. That sentence said by Ms. Cramm's niece Susan kept going through my head. "I like smoking pot and I don't want to hear anything bad about it." It wouldn't any more be just a matter of how I'd get my sister to stop smoking. It would be also a matter of how I could get her not to make me begin.

Linda was leaning back against the black pillows, inhaling the smoke deeply—like she'd shown me. She seemed very glamorous there in the flickering candle-light, with the soft guitar music spreading out in the room. I could see how those movie stars in the 1930s had gotten a lot of women started on cigarettes. It looked enticing and peaceful. She exhaled the smoke, and I could see it wafting across the softness of the candlelight. In fact, she seemed so relaxed and pleas-ured that it suddenly made me want to start in right then. After all, it would be the best way to get really *in* with my sister.

If I *didn't* have Corinne as my best friend anymore, I might just need to be close to Linda.

When she had tried on my blouse yesterday, I'd felt so jealous of her. Well, here was my chance to begin to be like her. If that's what I wanted.

Then—just as suddenly—what had looked so ap-pealing turned scary. If the drug changed Linda, then who *was* Linda? And who would I be if I was stoned? Right now I was confused enough about who I was. What did I want with another influence coming in and making what I think is me, not me?

"You don't have to come back," Linda said. "You don't have to start now if you don't feel you're ready yet."

"Oh—I'll be back," I heard myself saying.

If Linda had tried to force me into it, I would have said, "I don't know if I want to!" But with her saying it was my choice and being so nice about it, it made me feel obliged. Especially after all the trouble she'd gone to setting up this special environment for my birthday-present presentation.

Another thing: if Mom was getting close to Clive Anderson, that could mean she'd be further away from me. So I'd *better* not cut myself off from this best road to closeness with my sister!

"You forgot your present," Linda said as I stood in the doorway watching her.

"Oh," I said. "Well—could I leave it with you? You're more experienced in hiding all that stuff. If it was in my room Mom might find it."

"Sure," said Linda. "I'll keep it for you. In back of my stereo—if you ever want it when I'm not here. That's where I keep all my stuff."

"Good," I said. "Thanks." Then, in case I didn't sound grateful enough for all the thought and trouble she'd gone to—getting me that hand-painted Indian box instead of some junky plastic stash box, and getting me specially good birthday pot and all, I added, "Thanks a lot!" But it didn't come out sounding right. It came out the way you say it when someone gives you a big insult without even meaning to. And you answer, "Thanks a *lot!*"

But I guess Linda was too taken up with the joys of inhaling to notice. She just gave me a kind of lazy wave and said, "Shut the door, will you?" as I went out of her room.

I shut her door softly. But when I got back to my own room I shut the door very firmly and loud. Like I was saying to myself and to Linda, "Thanks. But no thanks!"

Then, even though I didn't have a history test, I started studying history. I thought I'd better, in case Linda should wander in and look over my shoulder to see what I was doing. She does that sometimes. She seems *amused* at the way I do my homework assignments. Like it's *cute* of me. I mean she obviously thinks I'm kind of jerky to try to get A's. All she tries is to get by.

Tonight the Ancient Romans seemed further away in time than ever. It was hard to care or even concentrate about what happened in the days of the Roman Empire when I was so worried about all the things that were happening to me right *now*. We were studying the *rise* of the Ancient Roman Empire. Next month, Miss Phelps had told us, we'd be studying its fall. I wondered whether the fall had anything to do with the Ancient Romans taking drugs. Once when I was home sick with a virus I heard some doctor on a morning talk show saying that the national epidemic of pot and PCP and uppers and downers among our nation's youth could cause the fall of our great U.S. civilization. Unless there was a turnaround right away. That word *epidemic* stuck in my mind because until then I'd more or less thought it was mostly something that just happened to be going on a lot in *our* school.

I kept turning the pages of the history book, trying to press the facts into my head. But not doing too good a job of it. I'd read a page through with my eyes. But my mind would be worrying about other things. Mostly how I was going to handle the matter of Linda and my new birthday paraphernalia kit. But also worrying about what I would do if Roger started rolling a joint in the movies on Saturday and passing it down the aisle to my birthday guests. And I was just plain worrying too about how the birthday party would go. Would Corinne be busy talking to other people; making it obvious to everyone that we weren't best friends anymore? Would Francene be clamping onto me like a leech so I couldn't be really free to be with the other kids? Would people think it was strange that I'd invited Jimmy? I didn't even know his last name! And would he turn out to be one of those fresh, stupid types who breaks a party instead of making it?

And then there was my Mom and the thirty thousand research reports. And Dad and his coming new baby, which would make me not his youngest anymore so I'd be even more forgotten about by him than I already was.

Sitting there thinking of all these things like Miss Gloom and Doom it was hard to imagine how I'd been so almost-happy just a couple of hours ago.

Suddenly I heard a terrible scream. And a crash of glass. It came from Linda's room.

11

I ran into Linda's room.

Then *I* screamed.

My sister was standing by the window, holding a lighted candle in a wine bottle. And something or somebody had broken the window. A big gashing hole of black night showed through.

When I screamed, Linda turned to me. It was Linda. But it wasn't. The candlelight lit her face and there was this strange glare in her eyes and this plastered stiff smile on her mouth. Then she said, "Get away!" And she threw the wine bottle right at me.

I screamed again. Screamed her name. The candle she threw at me went out. And the bottle didn't hit me. But the other candles still were lit. They made big shadows. Linda saw them too. She said, "They're after me. The shadows are after me!" And she leaned out through the jagged spears of window glass.

I was sure she was going to fall out the window. Or throw herself out. I raced across the room and grabbed her by her shirt and her hair and pulled her back in. But when I pulled her a piece of glass cut her face and her cheek was all bleeding.

"Get away from me," she said, in a low crazy-sounding voice. And she shoved me away so hard that I staggered back and fell down. She picked up another candle in a wine bottle, and glared at me as though she was going to slug it at me and knock me out.

I was so terrified that I was like frozen there on the floor. But when she got close and lifted up her arm with the wine bottle in her hand, I grabbed at her legs and pulled her over. And she fell. Then she started screaming that the shadows were coming after her and I shouldn't leave her alone. I scrambled to my feet and started to run out of the room. She was shouting that the shadows would get her. The shadows would murder her. I looked at the window. *She* must have broken it. Maybe if I left her alone she'd jump out. Without even thinking what I was doing, I did it. I shoved the bureau in front of the window. It's a very heavy bureau. I don't know how I moved it. Where I got the sudden strength. But I did. And when I turned around, Linda was squatting by the wall, crying. I didn't know if I should go to her and try to comfort her. Or whether she'd try to brain me again with the wine bottle, which she still was holding. Or *what* I should do.

And then she started hitting her head against the wall. And moaning. Clunk. The sound of her head against the wall. Then moan. Clunk. Moan.

"Linda!" I screamed out. "Stop! You'll hurt your brains."

But she kept right on. Clunk. Moan.

I raced out of the room, closing the door behind me, so maybe she'd think it was locked and wouldn't come out after me. Then I ran downstairs and into the sewing room, which doesn't have a lock on the door. And I picked up the telephone receiver. But I was so scared and so not-knowing-what-I-was-doing that I knocked the telephone off the top of the washing machine and it fell with a big clatter, scaring me even more.

I was afraid to put the light on to dial. Afraid

Linda would see the crack of brightness under the door, and come after me and kill me. But I couldn't dial without any light. So I switched it on and I dialed Dad's number. Then I switched the light off again.

I stood there in the total darkness, which seemed to be filled up by the sound of my heart thumping. But really, I guess, the only sound was the telephone—that steady soft burring sound that comes when the phone rings and rings and no one answers because there's no one home.

I began to cry. I had no idea on earth where my Mom was with this Clive Anderson. I couldn't start phoning around to all the restaurants. Maybe they'd gone to a movie. My only relatives live in Detroit. Should I call Corinne's mother? Or the police? Or the hospital? Suddenly I felt like I was in one of those TV programs with crime and stuff. I didn't feel like me at all. Emergency Room. Hospital Emergency Room. That was what people called. I dialed telephone information. I said, "Hospital Emergency Room."

"What hospital?" the information lady asked.

"*Any* hospital." I was really crying hard now. The feeling of being in a television drama had gone as fast as it had come. I was only me again. And I didn't know what I was doing, or what to do. And meanwhile my sister was upstairs maybe knocking her head against the wall, or maybe moving the bureau and jumping out the window.

"Honey," the information lady asked, "stop crying. Tell me where you live. What's your address?"

I told her. And she said, "Southside General is the

closest hospital to you." And she gave me the number.

I wrote it down on the pad that said Fairbanks Real Estate on the top. Then I dialed. When the other end answered, "Southside General," my voice burst out through my tears:

"Emergency Room. It's a terrible emergency."

After a minute a man's voice came on and I told him how my sister had gone sort of crazy and tried to kill me and how she was banging her head against the wall.

"Do you know if she's taken anything? Drugs?"

"No. Nothing."

"Does she use angel dust?" he asked. "PCP?"

"All she does is smoke pot," I said. "And she drinks wine."

He asked our address and said, "The ambulance will be right over."

"What should I do?" I almost screamed it at him. "Should I go back to her, or what?"

"If she's smoked pot laced with PCP," he said, "you'd better just sit tight till we get there. People do weird things sometimes when they've had some dust. We don't want two customers when we get there." Then he said, "Where are your parents?"

"Divorced. And out."

"You're there all alone?"

"Yes, alone. And I'm just little. I'm only eleven."

"Okay," he said. "Look, lock yourself in a room. We're on our way. We'll be there in five minutes."

Linda's room and the bathroom are the only ones with locks on the door. So I hung up the phone and I rushed upstairs to the bathroom. And I locked myself in.

Linda's room is right next door to the bathroom. I could hear her, and it made me so scared I felt dizzy. She had stopped thumping her head on the wall. Now she was screaming out, "Get those mice away. Get them off me. The flies are attacking me. Stop it. Help me. Oh, help me somebody. I can't move my arms. My arms are numb. Stop it. Get the mice away from me."

I'd been sitting on the edge of the bathtub in the dark. But I felt so faint with fear that I sat on the cold floor. Then I took a bath towel and hugged it to me. And I used it too to wipe my tears. And I kept taking big deep breaths so I wouldn't faint. What if I fainted and didn't hear the doorbell when it rang?

Finally, I heard it.

So did Linda. She screamed. "They're coming for me. They're after me." I heard her open the door of her room and run down the stairs.

Then I opened the bathroom door. And I stood at the top of the stairs. The bell rang again, longer. Someone knocked hard at the front door and a man's voice called out, "Hospital, Emergency."

Linda yelled, "No!" She fled into the kitchen. I thought of the knives hanging in their wooden rack by the side of the stove. "People do weird things sometimes," the emergency man had said.

I raced down the stairs and opened the front door.

Two men in white coats came in. And both said at the same time, "Where is she?"

I pointed to the kitchen. But I stayed there by the door, ready to escape into the night if she came after me.

I heard the two men trying to talk to her calmly. "It'll be okay," they said. "We're here to help you. No one's going to hurt you. We're not after you. We're here to help you."

But Linda kept screaming, screaming words. Single words. "Don't! Help! Please! Stop! HELP! DON'T!"

One of the men said in a loud stern voice, "Put down the knife!"

I kept standing there by the door. I didn't fall down. But I kind of blanked out with fear.

And then Linda was being walked out by the two men. She was between them. Each was holding hard to one of her arms. And she was struggling and kept screaming out those shrilly single words. "Help. Don't. Please. Stop. Help."

"If you don't quiet down," one of the men told her, "we'll have to call the police."

"*Why?*" My word shot out like a bullet.

"If we can't handle her, we'll need handcuffs," the man said to me. "The police have handcuffs."

"I think we can make it without the cops," the other man said. Meanwhile, they were walking Linda out the door. She began kicking at them and she kept on screaming. They got her to the open back of the ambulance. One of the men jumped in. He yanked her up, while the other shoved. They got her inside. Then the second man climbed in. The ambulance back door slammed closed.

And I just stood there.

It was cold. I felt frozen. But not with the night air. Frozen with the horribleness of what had happened. Frozen with the sound of my sister's crazy screaming from inside the ambulance.

Then the door opened a little. One of the men jumped out, and walked over to me. He was black. The other was white. They both were young. That's all I saw about them.

"I understand your parents are out," he said.

I nodded.

"Do you have a friend you can stay with till they get home?"

"I want to come with my sister," I said.

"Okay then. Leave a note for your parents. Tell them to come to Southside Hospital Emergency as soon as they get home."

I ran back inside. I wrote a note on the Fairbanks Real Estate pad.

Dear Mama:

I've gone with Linda to the emergency ward of the Southside Hospital. She didn't feel too good so I called the ambulance. I'll wait there with her till you come.

Love Jody

P.S. I hope you and Mr. Anderson had a nice time.

I put the P.S. in so she wouldn't feel guilty or ashamed if Mr. Anderson was there when she read my note. I didn't want him to think that I blamed my mother for her not being with us when the emergency happened.

I left the pad right by the front door. And I put the entranceway light on. That way she'd see the note as soon as she walked in.

The ambulance man was waiting for me on the steps.

I slammed the front door behind me.

"Got your key?" he said.

Oh God! I'd rushed out, never thinking about the key. I guess he saw that from the look on my face. "Well, never mind," he said. "Your parents will be coming along pretty soon. They'll have the key." We walked over to the ambulance. "Would you rather ride up in front with me? Or in the back with your sister?"

Now she was screaming curses. Terrible words I didn't even know she knew. She wasn't my sister.

"It's safe," the man said. "If you want to sit back there with her. We've got her strapped down to a stretcher."

"I want to sit up front with you," I said.

"Fine." He sort of tousled my hair. Then he opened the door to the front of the ambulance. "In you go," he said. And I climbed in. Then I began shivering.

He got in the other side. And he looked at me. Maybe he didn't see that I was shivering, because it was dark in the front of the car. But he did see that I'd forgotten my coat. "Here," he said. He took a wool blanket down from its place at the top of the seat. "Put this around you so you don't get cold."

I did. But I kept on shivering.

My skin didn't feel cold anymore. But my insides did. All the time that I was talking to this ambulance driver I kept hearing my sister screaming in the back. I talked a lot and I listened very hard to the things the driver was saying. I tried my best to shut out the sound of her screaming. But how can you do that?

I knew that I'd keep hearing the sound even long after she had stopped.

The ambulance driver told me that his name was

Gus. "Well," he said, "my real name is Basil. But what kind of a weirdo name is that? So everyone calls me Gus. My parents don't know why they named me Basil. They just thought it sounded like a fine name."

"Maybe they saw some old movie on TV with Basil Rathbone in it. Just before you were born."

"Yeah, maybe," he said. "But I'd rather they would have seen Clark Gable, or one of those other joes. I don't even know how I got the name of Gus. But that's the one that sticks."

Suddenly I thought of how one hour ago I was sitting at my desk trying to learn about Ancient Rome and worrying about such regular things as how my party would go. And suddenly here I was in the front seat of an ambulance with my sister screaming in the back and strapped down to a stretcher. And I was discussing with a perfect stranger how he got his two first names.

Suddenly he asked me whether I knew what kind of drug—or drugs—my sister was using.

"Well—pot," I said.

"Does she lace it with PCP?"

"What's PCP?"

"Phencyclidine. It has a lot of street names. Angel dust. Rocket fuel. Superjoint. Goon. Hog. DOA."

"DOA? Dead on arrival?" I knew that term from the hospital shows on TV.

"Yeah," Gus said. "Can you imagine anyone paying good money for a drug called DOA? Another cheerful name it has is killerweed. Because it can cause numbness in the arms and legs. It can make people *feel* dead. It's also called elephant tranquilizer. Because that's what it used to be used for. Elephants."

"I don't think my sister would have put that stuff

in the pot," I said. "At least not in what she was smoking tonight. It was pot she got for me for my birthday present. She was starting me off with my first lesson in how to roll a joint and all. I'm sure she wouldn't have started me off on killerweed elephant tranquilizer."

"Birthday present!" Gus said, as though he was spitting out the words.

"In fact," I told him, "she made a big point of saying that this was very good pot. The person she'd bought it from said it was something—special."

He gave me a quick side look. Then his eyes went back to the road. "Special, huh? A lot of these creeps doctor up low-grade marijuana with PCP. They sell it as good stuff. High-grade pot. They charge a high price. And the kids don't know what they're getting. Or getting into." Again he looked at me. "Did you smoke any?"

"No," I said. And I felt my insides all shriveling up with horror. If it hadn't been for Ms. Cramm and what she happened to teach us today, I might have smoked the joint that Linda rolled for me. The joint she had smoked instead of me. In fact, I almost surely would have. She was trying to be so nice and close and really helpful to me. And I would have wanted to do what I could to keep her like that.

If I had smoked the joint, it might have been *me* breaking the window and banging my head and tied down on a stretcher screaming in the back of the ambulance.

"She's got more of this stuff at home," I told Gus. "Can the hospital find if it's got PCP in it?"

"Sure," Gus said. "Tell your parents where she keeps it. Have them bring some to the hospital. The toxicologist will analyze it. Could be it's laced with LSD. But I'll lay my bets on PCP."

LSD. PCP. No wonder I didn't want to grow up. Right now I wished I was right back all the way to ABC. And safety.

"It's a real bummer," Gus said. "Like Russian roulette. You never know when it'll really hit you. Or how hard. Even a small dose—one you don't even know you're getting—can turn you into a raving maniac like your sister back there."

I felt insulted that he'd call Linda a raving maniac. Even though, impersonally speaking, that's just what she sounded like. I tried to turn the subject away from my sister. "Where does it come from?" I asked. "This PCP. What country grows it?"

He snorted. "What country? The good ol' U.S. of A. That's what. What *county*, you might as well ask. It's all over the place. And it doesn't *grow*. It's made. By creeps. They even publish the formula for making it in these druggy magazines. These legal rotten magazines that are helping to ruin a whole generation of our young kids. For what ends? For the holy buck!" He laughed a little. The saddest, bitterest laugh I ever heard. "Excuse me for sounding off like this," he said. "You bring in enough nice young kids like your sister, and it gets to you. Right in the guts. Sometimes I think I should quit the ambulance and join the police force. Do something about trying to stop it, where it's made."

"Where is it made?" I had to keep the conversation going. It was the only way to try to blot out my sister's screams. In the pauses between talk, the sound shook right through my body.

"Where's it made?" Gus said. "In cellars. In

trailers. Any hidden place. And some not so hidden. Last Wednesday the police found a PCP laboratory right above the Record Stop on Grove Street."

The Record Stop! I'd been there often. Mostly with Corinne. We'd flip through the files in different categories: rock . . . pop . . . jazz . . . blues. . . . And we'd discuss what records we would buy if we could afford it. And right upstairs people had been making this PCP! Maybe some of the very same PCP that was in the birthday-present pot Linda had bought.

It was like the grown-up world—or some of it—was in a conspiracy against kids. Instead of protecting us, they were busy making money off us. We were fooled into buying things just because we didn't know; things that could turn us suddenly into screaming maniacs like Linda.

I hadn't cried during all this time. And when this new thought hit me, I didn't cry either. Because it seemed that all my natural tears had shriveled up inside me. Dried by horror.

"Well, here we are," Gus said.

The ambulance turned in the hospital driveway, swerved around the corner of the building, and drew up in front of the neon sign that read, EMERGENCY ENTRANCE.

12

They carried my sister Linda through a big room where a lot of people were sitting on benches. She was still screaming. Not any words now. Just long, torn screams.

I followed behind the stretcher. It was the first time I'd seen how they'd strapped her down. She was writhing around. But she couldn't get loose.

Even in a nightmare I couldn't have dreamed up anything so terrible. These big thick straps over her. And my sister's shrieks cutting through the room where everyone was sitting so quietly. Naturally, all the sitting people stared at her. And at me, walking behind her.

We came to a gate, and a uniformed guard said, "You wait here, miss."

"But she's my sister," I told him. "I have to go with her."

"No kids are allowed in Emergency," he said. I could hear in his voice how he was sorry for me. "Where's your Mom and Dad?"

"I don't know," I said. "I have to go with her. Where are they taking her?"

By that time Linda and the two ambulance men had already disappeared. At least, disappeared from view. I still could hear her.

"Look," the guard said. "Go over to the desk. The nurse will need to get information from you."

So I went. The nurse took out some forms and I gave her information. Linda's name, address, age. I explained that one of our parents lived here in town and the other didn't. And I gave both addresses and telephone numbers. I also told the story of the special birthday pot.

The nurse asked me three different times if I knew what other drugs my sister took. And if she drank. I said as far as I knew she only smoked pot. "She doesn't like the taste of whiskey. But sometimes she drinks sweet wine. And beer."

The nurse wrote it all down. Then she told me to phone my mother and father, and to keep on phoning till someone answered. "They better get over here fast," she said.

"Is my sister going to die?" In the ambulance this thought had kept shoving at the back of my brain. But I wouldn't let it come as far as words. Now that I'd said the words I was more terrified than ever.

The nurse looked at me, and shrugged. "Probably not," she said. "On the other hand, I don't know what she's really taken. Or how much. We had three OD's in here last week. DOA's. So I'm not promising anything."

More terrible initials. "What's OD?" I asked.

"Overdose. Drugs. Why you kids with a nice soft life want to muck it up in the worst way, I do not know." She sounded furious. At me.

I thought of telling her that I'd never even tried pot and that I certainly didn't ever plan to. Not now. But an old man came up behind me and she turned to him and started asking him the same kind of questions she'd asked me. Name. Address. Insurance. So I just said, "Where's the telephone?" She pointed to the back wall. There were three phones, just out in the open where everyone could hear your conversation.

When I got back there I realized I didn't even have a dime in my jeans. Nothing but a crumpled paper handkerchief, a bus pass, and some peanut shells. Since the nurse had been quite obnoxious and the security guard was nice I went back to him and asked if he would lend me a dime for the telephone.

He gave me a dime, plus another thirty-five cents. "In case you want to get yourself some candy from the machine," he said.

I thanked him and bought some cheese wafers with peanut butter in the middle. I suddenly realized that, despite everything, I was hungry. Mom had left some hamburgers for us in the refrigerator. But with all that had been going on, I'd naturally forgotten about eating. Now it was ten past nine.

I ate all of the crackers. The peanut butter made me thirsty. But I didn't dare ask the security guard to lend me more money for soda. So I drank some water at the fountain. And while I was drinking, I realized that I didn't hear my sister screaming anymore.

Maybe they had wheeled her away to some far-off place where her screams wouldn't be heard by the people in the waiting room. Or maybe she had stopped screaming because—she was dead.

Suddenly the frozen tears all melted in a burst. And they flooded out of my eyes and my nose. I couldn't stop crying. At the telephone, I had to keep wiping my eyes so that I could see to dial. No one answered at our house. I didn't expect Mom to be home at nine o'clock. Maybe she wouldn't be home until midnight.

I tried calling Dad.

Oh, thank God! Somebody picked up the phone.

Diane. Well, she was better than nobody.

I tried to tell her what had happened, only I could hardly talk because of my crying. But she got the message. "Just give me the name of the hospital," she said, very firmly.

"Southside General. The Emergency part."

"Wait right there. I'll be with you in twenty minutes." And she hung up.

I'll be with you in twenty minutes. The words sounded so beautiful. Even if it was only Diane that was coming. Where was my Dad? Maybe he'd be coming too. *I'll* be there, she'd said. But at least she was grown up and sort of part of our family. And I wouldn't be all alone with this anymore.

It took her a half an hour. I kept my eyes straight on the door, which said EXIT over one part and ENTRANCE over the other. There were plenty of people in the waiting room that I could talk to. But I didn't want to. Since I'd come in behind Linda they'd know that she was my sister. They'd probably ask me what drugs she took. And I was afraid they'd launch off into stories of kids they knew who'd OD'd or gone off their rockers from drugs. And I wanted to try to get away from the subject. Not to go into it deeper. So I sat on a bench by the back, where I could be almost alone.

When Diane rushed in, I jumped up and ran to her.

The first thing she did was to hug me; put both arms hard around me and hugged so hard. I looked up at her face. She was beautiful. To me, anyway.

She smiled. "Don't worry, honey. Everything's going to be okay."

The nurse at the information desk called out, "Mrs. Jordan?"

Diane turned, and nodded.

"Come over here, please," the nurse said in a very bossy way.

"I need some more information about your daughter," the nurse said. And Diane had to explain how Linda wasn't her daughter, and she had less information to give the nurse than I did.

"But I would like to see Linda," Diane said firmly. "And I'd like to speak to the doctor."

"Where is the child's father?" the information nurse asked.

I'd been wondering that myself.

"Out of town," Diane said.

The nurse gave her a look that said, *That figures*.

I didn't want Diane to think they were all so mean here, so I led her over to the security guard and Diane repaid the forty-five cents he'd lent me. Then she gave me some more coins to buy more dinner from the machines. And the security guard let her through the wooden gate, the entrance to the Emergency Room.

On the other side of the gate Diane turned and said, "I won't be long, honey. I promise."

"That's okay," I said. "Be as long as you need to be."

Then I went to the slot machines and bought myself some bouillon, a ham and cheese sandwich on rye, a small tin of tomato juice, a packet of potato chips, and, for dessert, an Eskimo Pie on a stick. I brought them all back to my place on the back bench and had a picnic by myself. I wasn't really hungry anymore. But it helped to do something. And eating was the only thing I could think of to do.

Diane wasn't gone long. In fact, I hadn't even finished my dinner by the time she came out again.

She sat down on the bench next to me. "Linda's sleeping."

Sleeping! Oh, God. Thank God. Sleeping. Not dead.

"Is she better? Can we bring her home?"

"When they think she's all right, she has to be seen by the psychiatrist. If he dismisses her, she can go home."

"Oh, Diane," I said, "it was so awful. It was the awfullest thing I ever saw."

"I know, honey." Even though I was holding the ham and cheese sandwich, she took my hand in both of hers. I learned then that hugs and holding can speak so much deeper than words.

"Will she be okay Saturday for my birthday?"

Diane smiled a little. "The doctor said he couldn't make any predictions. They're not even sure yet what was in the pot. But that can be analyzed when your mother brings it in."

"She didn't know there was *anything* in it," I told Diane. "I'm sure of that."

"I'd like to have whoever sold her that stuff arrested," Diane said fiercely. Then she stood up. "Come on, sweetheart, I'll take you home. To your house. We'll wait there for your mother."

I told her then how I'd locked myself out, and we decided to go to the Sweet Shoppe for an ice-cream soda.

As we left the hospital I said, "What if Linda wakes up and no one of her family is here? Maybe we should stay."

"If there was any chance of that," Diane said, "nothing could make me leave here. But the doctor assured me she'd be in a sort of coma sleep for another five hours. At least. Which certainly gives us time for an ice-cream soda."

It wasn't until we were in the car that I thought to ask about Dad.

"He's at a sporting-goods convention in Detroit," Diane said. "The cheese store isn't the blazing financial success we'd hoped for. So your father's investigating the possibilities of opening a sporting-goods store."

"Will you have bicycles?" I asked.

She laughed. "I'm afraid we're a long way from stocking the merchandise," she said. "But I suppose if we go ahead with it, we'll have bikes. After all, they're a popular item, wouldn't you say?" She looked at me.

I nodded.

"Especially popular with eleven—or twelve-year-old girls," said Diane. Then she gave me this little smile.

I smiled back. I wondered how come I used to hate her so much. Well, because my father left us for her. But at least now I could begin to understand why.

First we drove past our house to see if Mom was home yet. But it was only ten o'clock and, naturally, no one was home. The house was dark. And no one answered the bell. So we went on to the Sweet Shoppe.

We sat in a booth far to the back. I ordered a

coffee soda with two scoops of chocolate ice cream and a whipped-cream topping.

"Same for me," Diane told the waitress. Then she looked down at her front, which did look rather protruding. "Baby, forgive me," she said. And she laughed a little. "I'm supposed to be on a diet," she told me. "And double-scooped ice-cream sodas are not on the recommended list for pregnant ladies."

Maybe she brought that up because she sensed I didn't want to talk about drugs. And freaked-out sisters. Not just then, anyway. So we talked for a while about the baby that she was having.

As we sat there discussing the way she was redecorating the guest room as a nursery, I noticed that two kids in the booth across from us had lighted up a joint.

Seeing them, I suddenly knew that at least one good thing had come from this night. I now had a very solid reason to do what I wanted to do. Which was—not to smoke grass.

If anyone tried to get me to try a "j," I'd just need to tell them what had happened to my sister when she'd bought me this great stuff for my twelve-year-old birthday present. I was relieved to have settled the matter in my own mind. Maybe that was the real birthday present my sister had given to me.

And probably what had happened would scare Linda enough so that she wouldn't turn off when I told her some of the scary things we were learning about pot in the class projects. And maybe she'd stop smoking it.

I decided I'd add this into the nightly prayers that I sometimes say when I'm in bed alone in the dark.

Diane saw me looking at the boy and girl in the

next booth. He had just passed the joint to her, and she was taking a deep toke.

Diane said, "Jody, don't ever think you have to do that in life to gain popularity or respect. Because if anyone's worth having as a friend, they'll respect you for wanting to be yourself."

I felt very relieved that she'd said this, even though it was something I'd just decided by myself. But it was nice having it confirmed by someone I liked. Loved.

The waitress set our sodas down on the table and I stuck a straw into the whipped cream and started sipping. It was delicious.

Suddenly I said, "It makes me so mad to see some of the kids in our school, how they're messing things up for themselves. They have nice families. They go to a good school. They have enough money. They have everything going for them. But they just make problems for themselves. They don't accept what they have. It makes me sick how they stay stoned all the time and louse things up for themselves and louse up their family life. They mess up everything. And pot psychs them into thinking that what's important isn't important. It makes me sick!"

I had never made such a boiling-hot speech in my life. I felt embarrassed.

But Diane said very quietly, "Bravo."

Suddenly I thought that maybe all the things I'd been worried about in turning twelve weren't that important. The period and body changes and all that didn't matter. What matters is *you*. If your period comes sooner, or later, what's the difference? It doesn't change who *you* are.

Before tonight, if I'd been in this Sweet Shoppe

with Corinne or someone, and I'd seen that boy and girl lighting up a joint, I'd have felt upset, confused. But now I know that—for me—I could handle it.

I could handle being twelve.

Diane smiled at me. "You know," she said, "after this experience, I think you're going to be one hell of a baby-sitter. The way you handled things tonight—I'm so proud of you. You did everything just right."

"I did?" I said.

"You did," she said. "You think you'll be able to baby-sit for us some weekends?"

"Sure," I said.

"Good!" said Diane. "Frankly, that's something I've been worried about. You hear so many stories of parents who come home to find their poor baby screaming away, and the baby-sitter just sitting there watching TV, stoned. But if you have this attitude, I'd like to hire you on the spot. Even prematurely."

"I certainly accept," I said. If I stayed with them weekends to baby-sit, I'd get closer to Diane. And closer to my Dad. It wouldn't be this stiff matter of trying to make conversation when he came for Visiting Rights and sat on the living room sofa. We'd talk about the baby and the sporting-goods store, and what kind of things I thought he should stock. Regular daily kind of talk; and we'd automatically come closer.

And maybe if Linda got off pot she might become more the way she used to be. And she and I would be close, the way we used to be. Long ago.

And then, instead of having just Mom for a family, I'd have two families. Both of them good ones; where I really belonged.

We finished our sodas and Diane looked at her

watch. "We'd better be getting back," she said. "Your mother may be home by now."

So, although I felt sorry to leave, I got up. And we walked out of the Sweet Shoppe together.

In the car, Diane asked about Steve. Was Linda still going with him? I told her yes—and how!

Then, since it was dark in the car and outside it, and everything seemed private and close between us, I told her what I'd never said to anybody: how the sounds they made scared me.

Diane put one arm around my shoulders, and sort of drew me over to her. "Honey," she said, "I don't know too many answers to things. But I do know this. You don't need to be scared about sex—if you take it slow. Just don't rush into anything. Wait till you're *more* than ready—for whatever you're going to do."

It was so great having a grown-up person I could talk to about these things. Maybe we could talk about *any*thing. Here I'd been hating her, for nothing. And she was turning out to be my best grown-up friend.

We pulled up by my house. But it was all dark. I was just about to say maybe we should go back to the hospital when the front door opened.

I heard my mother's voice: "Clive, please—don't. Please, just go!"

"Uh oh," Diane said softly. "You see, it's not only teen-agers that have problems along these lines."

The front door of our house slammed closed.

"It sounds as though your mother could use a little help," Diane said. We got out of the car, walked up the steps, and rang the bell. "Saved by the bell," she whispered to me.

The hall light went on suddenly. And Mom came to the door. She looked sort of mussed, and flustered.

"What on earth—" she exclaimed. She looked at Diane. "What are you doing here?"

"Didn't you see my note, Mom?" I burst out.

There it was, still on the floor, unread.

Mom picked it up. She went pale. She turned to Clive Anderson. "You'd better go. My daughter's in the hospital. What *happened?*" She turned back to me.

"The doctor's name is Gonzales," Diane said. "He wants you to contact him as soon as possible. But Linda's okay. Don't worry."

"Oh, God! What is it? Appendix? Something worse?" She ran to the phone. "*What happened?*"

"An—accident," Diane said. "The doctor will tell you about it."

"Do you want me to drive you to the hospital?" Clive Anderson asked my Mom.

She looked at him as though wondering what he still was doing here.

"I'll be glad to," he said. "My car's right outside."

"Well . . ." Mom hesitated.

"You don't want to drive there all alone."

"No," Mom said.

"I'll stay here with Jody till you get back," Diane said. "She should be getting to bed now. It's late."

"Yes," Mom said to me. "And you have school tomorrow."

In a minute they were gone, Mom and Clive Anderson.

And I, very tired suddenly, started up the stairs with Diane coming right along behind me.

13

When I got home from school the next day, Linda was back in her room!

And Mom was out with a real estate client.

I was so glad to see my sister. But I didn't know what to say to her.

"How do you feel?" I asked.

Linda shrugged one shoulder.

"Well," I said, "you look pretty good."

"I can't believe I broke that window," Linda said. "I don't remember anything about it."

The bureau was still shoved against the window. She must have looked to see why.

"Well," I said, "you weren't—yourself." The understatement of the century.

"I'm just so glad that you didn't take that stuff," Linda said. I could tell by her voice that she meant this very deeply. And it made me feel close to her. In fact, so close that I came into the room, instead of just standing there awkwardly in the doorway.

Then Linda walked over to me and she put both her arms around me. Just the way Diane had done. But because this was Linda, my sister, whom I really have loved so much for so long, it meant even more.

First I was so stunned that I just stood there, with my arms dangling down at my sides. And then I put my arms around her.

Linda made a snuffly sound. I looked up at her face. Her eyes were wet and tears were coming down her cheeks.

She released me, and laughed a little. But the sound came out more like crying. "You must think I'm pretty stupid," she said.

"For crying and all? No, I don't."

"I didn't mean for crying," Linda said. "I meant for—all."

Because I felt *I* might burst out crying if I stayed there, I said, "Well—welcome home. I guess I better go do my homework."

And I left her room.

That night when Mom came home she had A Talk with me. She showed me the report from the toxicologist. There *had* been PCP in the pot. And Linda hadn't known about it. "The doctor told me Linda was very lucky," Mom said. "She seems to have recovered quickly. But even so the drug can have certain on and off effects, maybe for months."

Then Mom asked me to level with her about whether I smoked pot or not. I was glad to be able to give her a Not. Then she told me if I had any problems or questions *ever*, about pot or any other drug, I should come to her and we'd talk it over. "Not that I know much about the subject," she said. "Probably you know more than I do. But it may help talking things out together. And if we have questions, we can go to the right people to learn the answers."

She ended our Talk by asking whether any of the kids coming to my party smoked pot. I told her Roger did. Maybe that was wrong of me. On the other hand, why should I have the whole burden of worrying about him getting stoned at my party and trying to turn my other guests on?

Mom said it would be better not to go to the pizza parlor. After the movies we should all come back here and have pizza and cake and ice cream in the dining room.

I felt relieved. Roger might not light up a "j" in the movies, because of the smell. The usher could spot him and ask him to leave. But the pizza parlor is a pot smoker's hangout. The spicy smell is heavy enough to be a cover-up.

The morning of my twelfth birthday was what I call a grizzly day. Gray and drizzly. But I tried not to think of this as an omen.

I took a long shower and washed my hair with some kind of nature shampoo which said on the bottle that it smelled as fresh as a sunlit waterfall. To me, it smelled like stale lemonade.

For some reason I felt very nervous. Once I saw an old Charlie Chaplin movie where he invited all these people to his birthday party and he had the table set up so beautifully for all the guests. And nobody came.

Why I thought that would happen to me, I can't say.

In fact, everyone did come.

And everyone brought a present. Each was wrapped up in fancy gift paper. I put them all in a pile on the dining-room table, to open after the ice cream and cake.

Then we all left for the movies.

It wasn't a very good picture. When I looked around no one seemed very involved.

At least, they weren't involved in the movie.

Linda was sitting in the back row with Steve. His arm was around her. And her head was against his shoulder. I wondered whether things would change between them, or whether *they* would change—because of what had happened.

Andrea Cohen and Roger were two rows ahead of me. His arm was around her, and they kept whispering together—so much that people around them would burst out "Shssssh!" in a cross way.

Francene was sitting on one side of me, and Pete on the other. Francene *started* whispering to me. But I said I was very involved in the movie. So she stopped. I was aware of Pete, on the other side of me. But he kept whispering to Jimmy, on the other side of him. He didn't seem aware of me at all.

And Corinne and Doris Oberbeck were sitting together in the side aisle.

I began to wish the movie, bad as it was, would go on and on. Sitting here in the dark, I felt safe. But I was afraid of what would happen when we went home. Everyone seemed to be two together. Corinne and Doris. Pete and Jimmy. Et cetera. The only one left for me to be two with was Francene. And I began to feel that all the others had come to my party as freeloaders. A free movie and food. Why not?

When the movie was over they showed the coming attractions for next week. Then we all got up and we met in the lobby.

"Come on, everybody," Linda said. "Next stop the bus stop."

(Mom had sent Linda along as a sort of chaperone. Not that we needed one. But maybe Mom thought Linda needed to *be* one.)

When we came from the movie lobby, I went through the door next to Corinne. I thought I'd better take the bull by the horns and get back on the track with her if I could. So, on the sidewalk, I said, "I feel that we're sort of drifting apart."

Corinne looked at me. "Yeah. I've noticed it too."

I took a deep breath inside me, and I got even more to the point. "I'm sorry that I didn't act nicer to you when you got your period. But I just—" I shrugged. "I don't know."

But Corinne knew. She knew how hard it was for me to say that. She shrugged. "I didn't care that much," she said. "I only told you because I thought you would like to know."

Then Francene came tagging up. I wanted to get away from her. I wanted to make it back to closeness with Corinne. But I understood how Francene must feel a lot of the time. The way *I'd* felt all alone in the movie dark. So I asked her how she'd liked the film. And, although I didn't much care what she felt about it, I pretended I was interested. And we walked on, the three of us, till we got to the bus stop.

I felt sort of good about not putting down Francene. To be truthful, last year I would have. If I felt down I felt I could get more up by putting someone else down. But when you put someone down, it *doesn't* make you any more up. All it does is increase the distance between you and the one you put down.

We all stopped to wait for the bus. And when it came Linda called out, "This is the bus." (We all knew which was the bus. But I was glad she was there, and doing her job.)

The bus is another two-by-two place. I wanted to sit next to Corinne. But with all these kindly thoughts I was having about Francene, what should I do? I hurried on the bus. Plunked in my fare. And sat down. Let come who may.

Corinne came. She sat beside me. And I knew it was going to be all right between us again. Then Francene came and stood above us, holding onto the strap. That made me feel good too. Like I was the center, instead of being all alone.

When we got home Mom had the pizza in the oven. She came out to greet us. "Everyone into the dining room," she said.

She had fixed it up into something special. There was a bright-red paper tablecloth on the dining-room table. And she had decorated the place with candles in wine bottles. I could have done without that reminder. One of those bottles had almost zonked me in the head. But with all the balloons bunching overhead, the wine-bottle candle holders sort of took the back seat as decoration.

We all sat down. There was a lot of laughing and talking. People seemed to be glad they were there. And when Mom brought in the pizza there was a lot of exclaiming. Sometimes pizza at home is soggy and bland. But this had been bought in the pizza shop, and Mom heated it up in the oven. It tasted great. Jimmy and Pete had three slices each.

At one point Pete, who was sitting next to me, took his napkin and wiped my chin. "You got cheese on your chin," he said. And he smiled at me.

I didn't know whether he smiled because he—liked me. Or because I looked funny with cheese on my chin. Anyway, I smiled back. Because I liked him.

Mom and Linda acted as waitresses. They poured out soda into paper cups. And they cleared away the paper plates and pizza crusts. Then they brought out two mounds of ice cream, chocolate and vanilla, and set them on the table. And—the grand finale—Linda came walking out of the kitchen carrying my home-made birthday cake.

Everyone burst out singing "Happy Birthday to You." Their voices sounded very loud and enthusiastic. As though they all really liked me. And I suddenly did feel that it was a happy birthday. Even though I now *was* twelve.

Linda set the cake in front of me. I looked at her. And she winked at me.

Then Mom bent over and kissed me on the cheek. She whispered so that only I could hear, "Happy birthday, my little girl."

I whispered back, "Thank you, Mama."

"Make a wish," Corinne said.

I closed my eyes. But instead of wishing, I had a thought: Being twelve isn't like jumping off a dock into deep water. Like Diane said, I can take things slow. No one's going to push me off. I'll walk in at my own pace. And when I'm ready, I'll swim.

Then I opened my eyes. I took a deep breath. And I blew out all the candles. Twelve. And one to grow on.

About the Author

Peggy Mann is a well-known writer whose by-line has appeared in most of our national magazines and who is the author of over thirty books, some for young readers and some for adults. Ms. Mann's novel *My Dad Lives in a Downtown Hotel*, a story of divorce, was dramatized as a television special, which was in turn nominated for an Emmy Award. The author's most recent Doubleday book for young readers is *The Secret Ship*, based on her best-known book for adult readers, *The Last Escape*, the true story of Ruth Klüger, who helped organize "the greatest secret rescue movement of all time," smuggling Jews out of Nazi Europe.